I can't get over how a person's life can be so boring for months at a time and then go crazy all of a sudden. It was two days before the Christmas break. Good. Ron Masten's dinosaur-sized brain knew that I was still seeing Samantha. Bad. I was still seeing Samantha. Good. She was going to Florida over the vacation. Bad. I was passing everything except geography, which I hate. Pretty good. I was sent to the office twice. Bad. My father hasn't come back. That may be good or bad.

Geez.

PAUL KROPP, a native of Buffalo, New York, holds degrees from Columbia University and the University of Western Ontario. He lives with his family in Ontario, Canada, where he is a teacher.

ALSO AVAILABLE IN LAUREL-LEAF BOOKS:

WILTED

Paul Kropp

LAUREL-LEAF BOOKS bring together under a single imprint outstanding works of fiction and nonfiction particularly suitable for young adult readers, both in and out of the classroom. Charles F. Reasoner, Professor of Elementary Education, New York, is consultant to this series.

Published by
Dell Publishing Co., Inc.
1 Dag Hammarskjold Plaza
New York, New York 10017

Laurel-Leaf Library ® TM 766734, Dell Publishing Co., Inc.

ISBN: 0-440-99396-2

RL: 5.3

Reprinted by arrangement with Coward, McCann & Geoghegan, Inc.

Printed in the United States of America

First Laurel-Leaf printing—February 1982

WILTED

Only wilts wear glasses. The only person I know and like at all who wears glasses is Bloop. And when you stop to think of it, he's a little wilted too.

"Mom, I'm gonna look like a wilt." We were walking up James Street to the optician. The wind blew up from the bottom of the street and pushed my hair back. I must have looked deformed.

"What is a wilt?" she said, not even slowing down.

"You know, somebody who's really out of it. It's like his whole personality got melted by a laser beam."

"Stop being so stupid, Danny. The reading specialist said that you need glasses. The school nurse said that you need glasses. So you're going to get glasses, even if you are going to look like this Wilt person."

She hadn't even listened. I hate it when somebody asks you a question and then doesn't listen to the answer. Teachers are like that, sometimes. My mother was like that, almost all the time.

"And these glasses are costing us a pretty penny, young man, money your father can barely afford."

This time I wasn't listening. Some gum got stuck to the bottom of my shoe. I could feel the lump it made under my big toe and knew it was making one foot stick to the street. I was probably walking like I just left the Jerry Lewis telethon.

When we walked up the steps to the optician, the wind blew my mother's coat around her so she looked like a beanpole. It also made the door smash when I opened it for her. She gave me a look, one of those looks. Why doesn't she give me some credit for opening the door? I mean, why should I bother playing the gentleman if she's just going to give me "the look."

When we got inside the door I checked to see if there was anybody I knew. If the Bloop or Ron Masten or Whitey were in the waiting room the kids at school would be laughing about my glasses before I even got them. Fortunately, there was nobody inside but a pretty senior-high-school girl with a scrunched-up face. If she wasn't squinting so hard she'd look almost as good as Samantha Morgan in my homeroom. I figured she was waiting for her glasses to come back and couldn't see properly. I felt relieved. That meant I could watch her all I wanted and she wouldn't know it. She'd probably be gone by the time I tried on some glasses and looked really wilted.

"We'd like to pick out some frames for my son. I have the prescription here." My mother spoke to an old man who seemed to have more hair growing out of his nose than out of his head. He smiled like an actor on a toothpaste commercial.

"Of course," he smiled, "this is a relatively low correction so you have a pretty free choice: metal frames, plastic, regular glass lenses, the lightweight plastic ones . . ."

"I think I should explain," my mother lowered her voice so I knew she was embarrassed, "cost is a consideration. We were thinking of something in a moderate range."

"I understand fully," he smiled.

I didn't believe a word of it. The optician was wearing a suit that probably cost more than our whole car. What did he know about it? If it started to rain while we sat in the office, the car wouldn't start when we got back to the meter. If it got really cold, we had to shoot ether into the carburetor and pray. One day when my brother Jimmy got in the back seat he put his foot through the floor. My father had to put some sheet metal over the hole and cover the floor with tar. And this optician with no hair and the expensive suit thinks he understands fully. I should have told him, look, buddy, you don't understand at all.

He pulled out two kinds of frames. One looked like the kind Clark Kent wears on "Superman" reruns. The other pair were made out of clear plastic and should have been worn by a boy genius on an after-school movie. Before I came I thought I would end up looking wilted, now I *knew* I would end up wilted.

"Which do you prefer, young man?"

"Yes, Danny. Which kind would you like? Here, let's try each of them on," my mother said and started to shove the Clark-Kents on my face.

"I don't like any of them," I said loudly. Then I remembered the pretty girl in the office probably had good ears even if her eyes couldn't focus beyond her big toe.

"Look, Danny," my mother was getting a little red

in the face, "I know you don't want to wear glasses, but you simply have to. The reading teacher says she doesn't want you back in class without some glasses. You know you can't really see properly. Now, all we're asking you is to make a choice."

I started looking around the room. There were all these displays of old people wearing glasses and flashing toothpaste smiles. There wasn't one person in the displays under thirty. Wait a minute, there was one picture of a kid who looked like he had just left the chemistry lab after discovering a cure for cancer. He wore the boy-genius frames. I hoped the kid was happy in his chemistry lab because with those glasses no girl would ever go out with him.

On a sunglass ad there was a lady who looked like the dumb reading specialist who started this whole thing. Mrs. Downey wore glasses that changed color with the brightness of the room light. Whenever I saw her she had just come in from outside so it took ten minutes before her glasses got clear enough for her to see anything. I didn't like her. She kept trying to pretend she was my friend. Not by putting her arm around me or anything, but in that sick way teachers have, "Now do you have any problems at home, Danny?" None of her business. Someday I'm going to ask her, "Mrs. Downey, do you have any problems at home that you'd like to talk about?" That'd fix her. I bet she does, too. She's divorced and tries to look like a model on the cover of *Cosmopolitan.* That's a laugh. She'd never even make the cover of *Reader's Digest.*

I'm still not sure how she figured out I needed glasses. Of course, I knew all along. For two years I knew that the print looked like squirming ants when I

tried to read a book. But I didn't tell anybody. I just
kept on reading the little-kid books with the big print.
Then old Mrs. Sporbeck decided I had "dyslexia" and
sent me off once a week to see Mrs. Downey when
she came to school. I remember when Mrs. Sporbeck
wrote "dyslexic" on my report card I thought it was
like dandruff until I looked it up.

"Young man, if I could suggest this pair." The optician pointed to the boy-genius frame. "It's very sturdy
and will stand up well to playing sports in school."

"What do you think, Danny?" My mother started
giving me the same toothpaste smile. I'll never figure
out why adults show their teeth when they really
want to hit you.

"I think you'll look quite handsome with them on,
Danny," the optician came in.

"Would you two stop ganging up on me." My
mother stared at me, but I didn't care. I looked right
at the optician and kept my eyes on the hairs that
stuck out from his nose. "And don't call me Danny.
You don't even know who I am."

The optician was still smiling but he had to work
harder to keep it up. Good. I put the glasses on and
looked at my face in the mirror. The kid who looked
back was wilted. The glasses covered up my eyebrows
and made my ears stick out. It was awful. I've always
said that you can never trust people if you can't see
their eyebrows and now I had no eyebrows. My ears
were bad enough before, now I looked like Mickey
Mouse.

"They're OK," I grunted.

"Very well, then," my mother said, looking relieved.
"We'll take this style."

"That's fine ma'am, we should have them ready in two or three days." The optician put the glasses back on the rack and made a note of the prescription.

When I got back into the waiting room, I could see that the squinting girl had left. That was too bad. I wondered what she looked like with glasses on and her face unscrunched. Maybe she bought contact lenses. Maybe I could too if they didn't cost two hundred dollars.

My mother and I didn't talk while we walked back to the car. I got back to it first and got in. My mother opened the other door and sat on the driver's side. She looked over at me and I knew she was going to do something. Then she slapped me, hard, on the cheek. The slap really stung, and I knew that my face was going red. I wanted to hit her back but I knew that my father would kill me if I did. I knew I couldn't hit her even if I didn't have a father. I wanted to cry like Jimmy would, but I was too old for that. So I set my teeth together and just stared at her.

"I never want to be embarrassed by you like that again." She was getting red in the face, now. "You were rude to the optician and to me. That's why I slapped you. You're fourteen years old and should know better."

"I didn't like the glasses," I said between my teeth.

"It's all that we can afford. I can't get you fifty-dollar frames. Your father just doesn't make enough money. Can't you understand? It's not easy for us, either."

Yes, I understood. I looked outside and watched the rain drip down the windshield. Nothing is worse than a cold rain in October especially when you know it will be snowing in a month.

My mother tried to start the car. The starter turned over, but the motor wouldn't catch. She tried again. And again. When the starter wouldn't turn at all, we both knew the car wasn't going to move.

My mother didn't swear like my dad would have. She was very controlled. She sat very still on the crackly vinyl seat, watching the rain hit the windshield. The raindrops were sliding down the glass, probably leaking into the engine and getting the wires and spark plugs wet. It was quiet while I sat there thinking about the water on the engine, the dead battery, and the lost spark. After a minute I turned and looked up at my mother's face. Her cheeks were wet.

2

The day I had to wear my glasses to school started off with my toast getting stuck in the toaster. First thing in the morning, everybody running around on tiptoes to keep from waking up my father, and the toast gets stuck. I felt like swearing at the top of my lungs, but I couldn't, so I turned to my brother Jimmy and said quickly, "Shit."

"What?" he said.

"Shishkabob. It's what you say when your toast gets stuck."

"Oh. Where's my Cheerios?"

Seven years old and the kid still can't get his own Cheerios. You'd think it took some talent. I made Jimmy his breakfast, pried out the black pieces of toast with a fork, and waited. We always spent a lot of time waiting for my sister Shelley. She got twice as much time in the bathroom as all the rest of us combined. Every morning she went in for a solid twenty minutes. I kept on expecting a miracle when she came out. The miracle never happened.

"Hurry up," I yelled through the bathroom door.

"Shut up!" she yelled back.

"Look, you better stop yelling or you'll wake Dad up," I yelled.

"Just keep your pants on."

"Ooh, ooh, ooh. I can't wait." I started jumping around on one foot making funny faces. Jimmy laughed and dribbled a Cheerio on the table. Then he laughed at the Cheerio.

"There," she said, opening the door. "All yours."

"Ooh, ooh, ooh, you're so beautiful!" I said with my Count Dracula voice. She just stared at me.

I locked the door and tried on the glasses. Not that bad, I said to myself. Almost distinguished. I made a distinguished-looking face in the mirror. The glasses made it easier to see the pimples on my face. Just what I needed. I gave up being distinguished and stuck out my chin to get at a pimple. What a way to start the day, stuck toast and a complexion like the surface of the moon.

I combed my hair so it covered up my flapping ears. When I left the bathroom, my mother was waiting.

"You woke your father up, you know."

"Well, Shelley was taking forever in the bathroom. I had to go."

"When are you going to grow up and start thinking about somebody other than yourself." She went off smiling, happy with her little lecture. I would have said something, but the glasses made me see some lines in her face I'd never noticed before.

The weather was fine for late October. I kicked

leaves while walking down to the Circle and sat down waiting for Bloop. Bloop's real name was Myron Rabinowitz, but he had gotten his nickname when Don Ready watched him walking down Vergil Avenue. Don said, "That kid looks like a Bloop." Everybody looked down and saw that Don was right: Myron was a perfect Bloop.

Bloop is smart. He's a lot smarter than kids who try to fight against a nickname. Bloop knew that throwing your time and energy away against a perfect nickname is like trying to fight the wind. I remember the day after Don named him, somebody came up to Bloop in the hall and said, "Hi, Bloop." Everybody was watching to see what he would do and the Bloop knew it. So he gave his huge grin, as if somebody just gave him a free Big Mac, and said, "Bloop? Bloop. I like it."

I saw Bloop and Crazy Charlie coming toward the Circle together. Actually Bloop was walking right behind Crazy Charlie, imitating the old man's step. It made me laugh. I waved at Crazy Charlie to make him come on over. After burnt toast, new glasses, and a lecture from my mother I needed something to cheer me up.

"Hey, y-you got some g-glasses," Crazy Charlie said, wiping the corner of his mouth.

"That's right, Charlie, and these are special glasses. They're telescopes, so I can see right into outer space. I'm gonna look for UFOs today." I knew Charlie would like this because he had told us two weeks ago that he went for a trip in a flying saucer. Bloop pretended he really believed him and got Crazy Charlie going.

"Y-you're k-kidding me."

"No, Charlie, I never kid you. You know those glasses that change from light to dark? Well, these work on the same principle. They can change from regular glasses into telescopes."

"How'd you get your mother to buy those?" Bloop joined in. "They must have been pretty expensive."

"Mother had to sell a few stocks, but, if I may quote her, 'Nothing is too good for my Danny.'" I pressed the side of the glasses and pretended to focus on something up in the sky.

"Do you s-see something?" Charlie asked.

"No, it was a false alarm. But I'll be checking the sky throughout the day."

"Come on, we've got to get to school so you can do your astronomy homework. Let's go." Bloop gave me a look, so I patted Crazy Charlie on the shoulder and took off.

Bloop didn't start laughing until we were a block away. Then his face crinkled up and he giggled through his teeth and his nose.

"Pretty good, huh?" I said.

"Yeah. And do you ever look terrible in those glasses."

"Really?" I said, my voice cracking.

"Well, maybe not terrible. You look like the sort of kid they'd put in an advertisement to sell chemistry sets."

"Sort of a boy genius," I offered.

"Yeah, but wilted."

The other kids in my homeroom didn't see me as I came in. I thought this might be a good sign. Sally the Browner was up by the chalkboard putting out stubs of chalk. This meant that Mrs. Edelstein was going to terrify her French classes with board work. Richard was busy telling Whitey a joke while Whitey sneaked cookies from the lunch bag in his desk. Rocky was talking to Joanne over by the flagpole. Mrs. Edelstein was blowing her nose and working on her grade book at the same time. She's the only person I've ever seen who always has a Kleenex in her hand. She must have a pop-up dispenser in her sleeve.

"Hey, look at Danny," Whitey yelled, spraying bits of cookie.

"Wow, what specs!"

"The dummy's trying to look like a brain."

"Did you get 'em out of a Cracker Jacks box?"

I tried my best to look dignified. I knew, all the way to school, that this was going to happen. I had tried to get ready. I kept a half smile on my face and said nothing. Then the Bloop turned on me.

"Doesn't he look like a boy scientist, just escaped from his fifteen ninety-five Gilbert chemistry set?"

Everybody broke up. They were just looking for an excuse to start laughing, and Bloop gave it to them. My friend. My best friend. My former best friend.

"You shit," I muttered.

"Easy boy, keep your cool," Bloop said over the laughter.

"That will be quite enough," Mrs. Edelstein broke in to cut off the laughing. "I don't need your rudeness to Danny at this hour of the morning or at any other time, for that matter. Peter White, lunches are to be eaten only in the cafeteria."

That's the worst thing, when the teacher has to stick up for you. Then you know that you've done something so dumb, or maybe that you just *are* so dumb, that you can't handle it yourself. Gerald Rosen, the class loser, was always having teachers stick up for him. It just made things worse. Now Mrs. Edelstein had made me another Gerald Rosen. Thanks a lot.

I really wanted to punch somebody, probably Bloop, but I knew that I couldn't. I tried to tell all the blood cells who were busy having a party in my cheeks that they were needed elsewhere. It didn't work. Not only did I feel embarrassed, but my red face advertised the fact.

"Hey, what's all the laughing about," came a low roar from the door. I knew by the voice that it was Ron Masten, all two hundred pounds of him plodding down the aisle toward me.

"I don't believe it. I don't *believe* it." Ron came up to my desk and stared at me. His lips were curled back in an awful smile that made his teeth look like a zipper across his face. When his smile turned into a laugh, his mouth would open crooked, like a zipper opening up from one cheek to the other.

"I don't believe it!" he shouted one more time for emphasis. I could see his stomach jiggling with the laugh that followed it.

I focused my eyes again on the papers in front of me and pretended to be doing some homework. Everybody knew that I was pretending—I never did homework before class—and that made it worse. What else could I do? Some days you shouldn't just stay in bed, you should Scotch-tape a pillow over your face.

While Ron's stomach was still jiggling, Samantha came in the door with Gerald Rosen. I don't mean she came in *with* that loser, but they happened to come in at the same time. I think I had worried about this moment more than any other. It's not even that I liked

Sam that much. In a lot of ways she's just out of my league. But what she would do was still more important than the noise from the other guys.

Ron went running up to her. He was too stupid to see that Mrs. Edelstein was staring at him or maybe he didn't care. I couldn't hear what he said because he whispered to Samantha, though a couple of kids nearby heard him and they started to laugh. Samantha looked over in my direction while I pretended not to see her. She stared for a second or two, then shrugged her shoulders and sat down.

I could have kissed her. Well, you know what I mean.

3

I like math. I like it partly because I'm good at it and partly because of this fantastic math teacher, Major Henry. Major Henry really was a major in World War II and he should probably retire. Some days I'm sure that he's senile. But other days he comes up with the most amazing stories.

One day he stopped in the middle of a lesson on the Pythagorean theorem to talk about booby-trapped toilets. He said that in the war the Germans used to leave dirty magazines in the outhouses. Some poor soldier would go out, drop his pants, sit on the toilet, and pick up the magazine. There was a wire connecting the magazine to a detonator. Boom. "The explosion would blow his ass right off," Major Henry said. Then he went back to the Pythagorean theorem.

Major Henry is sort of a philosopher, too. I remember the day Gerald Rosen asked him if the board work was important. Major Henry leaned back in his chair and didn't say anything while he cleaned his glasses. Then he leaned forward. "Gerald, the only thing that's really important is being able to tell the shit from the shoe polish." I thought he was joking then but I'm starting to understand a little more now.

Another thing I like about math is that Samantha sits right in front of me. Her last name is Morgan and mine is Morrison. It's nice. When I get bored doing math problems I can always stare at her curly hair. I mean, when you're sitting in math for almost an hour you need something to take your mind off the numbers.

It was late November when the first big math test came up. I wasn't too worried about it, but everybody else was. Even Ron Masten, who says he steals dynamite sticks to use for firecrackers on the Fourth of July, was a little shaky. He should be. He's really stupid.

I could tell that Samantha was nervous when she came in. She turned around right away and started talking to me. She doesn't usually talk to me when she's feeling good or has something better to do. But she was nervous. She was chewing gum, even though it's not allowed.

"I wish we could use calculators," she said.

"Who needs them. This way the problems will be easier. Using calculators is like having an open-book test. The teachers always make it harder." I checked to see if my pen worked by writing on my hand. I saw that Samantha had writing on her hand as well. "What's that?"

"The formula and some times tables."

"Times tables! You don't know times tables?"

"I guess I do. But I feel better if I have them written down." She smiled and I saw that her teeth were perfect. I wondered why girls always had perfect teeth while mine were crooked. A mystery. Probably the same reason they never have BO.

Major Henry was up at the front of the room stretching a rubber band. He was very carefully pulling the rubber band out about four inches and then letting it come back to normal size. Like I said, some days I think he's senile.

"Mr. Henry," Ron put up his hand, "is there something special about that rubber band?"

Ron was stalling. We all knew that. If he could get the major talking about his rubber band long enough, he might have to cancel the test. We had used that trick before.

"Right you are, Ron. Do you kids know that this rubber band is twenty-five years old?"

He looked around the room, holding the rubber band as if it were magic. We all shook our heads no. Ron made a face as if the rubber band's birthday was the most amazing thing he'd ever heard.

"Well, it is," the major went on. "My first year teaching I had this rubber band. You might say we're old friends now, both about ready for retirement. But neither of us will quit. You know why?" He paused. "Exercise."

"Exercise?" Ron stalled.

"Exercise. Every day I exercise my body and I exercise this rubber band. That's why I've been able to last so long. Your muscles are just like rubber, you have to exercise them every day so they'll stay pliable. I've been stretching this rubber band every school day for twenty-five years and it's almost as good as new. Just like me. Look."

He stretched the rubber band a bit. I couldn't look at it or I'd laugh, so I looked at Samantha's hair.

"Mr. Henry." Gerald Rosen waved his hand. "Don't forget about the test."

"Geez," Ron said under his breath. Everybody stared at Gerald and made a face as if he were a giant centipede. What a loser!

It was about halfway through the test when I saw that Sam was having trouble. She started scratching the back of her neck over and over. There's nothing wrong, of course, with scratching your neck during a test. So long as your other hand is writing. Sam was scratching her neck with her writing hand. As far as I could tell, the other hand was just sweating. I know the feeling well.

I shifted in my chair a bit and looked at the first couple of answers on her test sheet. All wrong. I thought about what I could do: set off the fire alarm, fake an epileptic fit, pretend there's a gas leak. I liked all these ideas but didn't have the guts or the talent. Samantha's problem was simple: she needed the answers. The solution was also simple: I started writing them down on a piece of scrap paper.

When I was finished, I folded the sheet up and put it in my palm. The Bloop looked over at me while I was folding and gave me a look. I stared back at him with a mind-your-own-business look, and he did. Then I raised my hand so I could go up to Major Henry's desk and ask him a question.

Walking up to Major Henry, I knocked the papers on Sam's desk with my jacket. A couple of sheets fell to the floor and I bent over to pick them up. When the sheets were back on her desk, there was one extra.

I went up front to ask some stupid question about problem 17.

I was worried for the rest of the test. Major Henry was too senile to notice anything, so he wasn't the problem. Whitey had been looking at the answers on Sally's paper during the whole test, and the major didn't say anything. But there was always the chance that one of the other guys would rat on me. It's always your friends who knife you in the back.

Sam didn't say anything to me in the hall, and I didn't want to talk to her. But in science, while Mrs. Shenker was going on about absolute zero, I caught Sam looking my way. At first I was sort of embarrassed. I thought maybe I looked funny, like the day a pimple started on my nose. But then my imagination started going crazy. Maybe my glasses really improved my looks. . . . The idea fell apart as soon as it got into my head. I spent most of the period confused.

When the bell rang, Sam came over to my desk while I tried to gather up my notebooks. I couldn't seem to get hold of the whole pile and felt pretty dumb with papers falling out all over.

"Thanks."

"It's OK. I owed you a favor, anyway."

"What for?"

"Couple of weeks ago. Never mind. Let's say we're even."

4

I had almost forgotten about the math test when I ran into Major Henry on my way to basketball practice. He waved and called me over.

"Yes, sir."

"Danny, I noticed you this morning rather ineptly trying to assist Samantha during the test."

I was frozen.

"While I may be senile, I am not yet blind. Now don't get upset. It's only a math test. Just how important is a math test, Danny?"

"I don't know, sir. Very important."

"No, Danny. You were right when you said you don't know and wrong when you said very important. What you have to learn is how to tell what's important from what's trivial. In your case, going after Samantha is probably more important than getting a good mark on today's test." He started smiling. "Do you understand?"

"I think so."

"You will. Anyway, I'm deducting twenty points from your mark for incorrectly assuming that I'm blind. But I'm going to let Samantha keep her ill-gotten marks as a gesture . . . a gesture toward absolute value." He started laughing. His big, open laugh spread down the hall and kids started looking at us. I mumbled a thank-you and headed to the gym.

When I left school after basketball practice, I was still confused. I watched the snowflakes fall, trying to figure out whether Major Henry was giving me advice or laughing at me. I was no closer to an answer when I reached the house.

Our car was gone. My father was probably on the afternoon shift for the week. The house was really quiet as I hung my coat up, and the kitchen was empty. My mother must have gone out.

The stairs creaked as I walked up to the bathroom. Going by Shelley's room, I could catch just a faint smell of grass. When she smoked she always left the window open so the smell wouldn't build up. I had once asked her why.

"So the ancient ones won't find out," she said.

"You think they don't know?"

"They don't want to know. If you weren't so wilted you'd understand that there are a lot of things people don't want to know."

So I knew that nobody else was home. Shelley never smoked, even cigarettes, when either my mother or father were home. I yelled to her through the bedroom door.

"Where's Mom?"

"Geez. Don't yell!"

"Can I open the door?"

"Yeah."

Shelley's room was a mess. Somehow she managed to trash it up right after my mother's weekly cleaning. Clothes were everywhere. There were some black-light posters on the walls with an ultraviolet lamp to make them glow. I thought that was really something when she first put them up. But I was younger then and didn't know that *nobody* still had black-light posters. The whole place smelled sweet, not from the grass, but from the incense she burned to cover the smell.

"Close the door, dummy."

Shelley was over by the window. She was leaning against the radiator in a way that probably left dents in her back. She wasn't smoking, but the mayonnaise lid she used as an ashtray was right next to her.

"Where's Mom?"

"Christmas shopping. She took Jimmy."

"What are we supposed to eat?"

"Polish steak."

"Yecch."

Shelley was half wrecked. I could tell by the eyes and the easy grin always about to break into a laugh. Her blonde hair was stringy and her skin got very pale in the winter, as if she was dying. Maybe she was. She coughed all the time.

"Want on?" She grinned at me and teased me with a joint.

"Get out." Some of the kids in my class smoke, but I always thought it was pretty dumb. I wanted a chance to grow up before I wrecked myself.

"Your choice. Sooner or later you will." She lit up.

"Why should I? You've been stoned off and on for two years now. What's it done for you? You've picked up one mangy boyfriend, almost flunked a year at school . . ."

"Shut up."

". . . and caused Mom and Dad a lot of grief."

"They don't know."

"Sure they do. Mom's not that dumb, you know. She went to college for a while. She knows that Mangy Bob's on something. I heard Mrs. McKirgen talking to Mom about him last week. You're causing some real trouble around here."

She got me mad. I didn't usually call her boyfriend Mangy Bob to her face, but the name was perfect. Bloop had made it up. Mangy Bob wasn't wilted, he just looked like he needed delousing and smelled like a perfume gone to hell.

"No, it's not me," Shelley looked glazed. "It's not me. The old man's been drinking more than ever. How long is Mom gonna put up with it? They should never have gotten married."

"That's your fault, too."

"Shit. What do you ever do around here but hide behind comic books and make everybody else feel guilty." She looked out the window. "Besides, I've been thinking about taking off. Getting out of here."

"To do what?"

"I don't know. Maybe go out west."

"You know what the trouble with you is, Shelley? You want to know? It's that you can't sort out what's important. You're nowhere."

"Yeah, how do you know?"

" 'Cause it runs in the family."

5

Jimmy and I have to share a bedroom. This didn't use to bother me, but lately Jimmy has been working on some wilted habits. He eats sunflower seeds in bed. He wants to talk before he goes to sleep. He blows his nose and stuffs the Kleenex under the mattress.

All these habits are pretty noisy, so the quiet that night was surprising. My mother was downstairs doing her back exercises before starting on *Thirty Days to a More Powerful Vocabulary*. Shelly was in her bedroom probably writing a letter to Mangy Bob who was on a "business" trip to Rhode Island. The radiators were knocking like they always do, and that was the only noise besides Jimmy eating sunflower seeds.

"Danny."

"Yeah?"

"What are you doing?"

"Reading."

"The Hulk?"

"Yeah."

"Do your Hulk voice."

I cleared my throat and let my jaw droop a bit. Then I read. "Hulk never *saw* such huge monster. It not big enough to hurt. *me*.. *Nothing* can hurt Hulk. . . . Nothing . . . and now Hulk prove it." I made some fight noises by grunting and hitting my pillow. "Monster is heavier and *stronger* than Hulk thought. Hulk will need all his strength. But . . . uunnhhh . . . Hulk win." Then I gave him the dying monster sounds.

"That's great."

"Yeah. Now go to sleep."

"Can't. I'm scared."

"Look. You're seven years old. It's after ten o'clock. Don't give me that line of BS about being scared. Go to sleep."

Jimmy shut up. I kept on reading about Hulk who was up against an interdimensional teleporter controlled by Maximus. When Hulk tried to fight against it, he was transported to another dimension. One swing and zap . . . right to the hidden citadel.

"Danny?"

"What now?"

"What if Mommy and Daddy got divorced?"

"Huh?"

"We've been reading this book in school about divorce."

"Geez. Is that what they do in second grade?"

"Well, what if they got a divorce?" Jimmy stretched out his arm and knocked his sunflower seeds on the floor.

"They'd just split up and live in separate houses.

We'd probably end up with Mom. That's what usually happens."

"You think they might?"

"No," I lied. "They've been married too long to split now." This was one of those lies I was trying hard to believe. I figured if I could believe it maybe Jimmy would, too. It's better than worrying all the time about something you can't control.

"Oh."

"Go to sleep."

"But they fight a lot. Just like the people in the book. Daddy even hits her sometimes."

"Don't worry about it. Go to sleep."

In five minutes Jimmy was snoring away, louder than the banging radiators. This was one of the things that bothered me about him. He asks an important question, gets a dumb answer, and he's happy. Me, I worry. His questions had made me jumpy. I didn't feel like reading and couldn't fall asleep. I pulled the pillow around and started hugging it. I tried to force my mind back to thinking about Samantha. In a few minutes that worked. I felt better and started dozing off.

I couldn't have been asleep very long when my father got in from work. The clunking of his safety boots on the floor woke me up from a light sleep. I heard him walk into the kitchen, which was almost directly under our room. His voice and my mother's came up through the floor.

"I'm surprised you didn't go out for a drink like you usually do."

"Didn't feel like it. Don't you want me home?" My father pulled a kitchen chair across the floor.

"Do you want to help wrap up some presents?"

"No, it's enough that I pay for them, isn't it? I got the bill from Robinson's today."

"I'm always glad to see the mail delivered. Neither rain nor sleet, you know."

"Would you stop the smart-ass comments when I'm trying to talk to you. You spent over a hundred dollars last month."

"It's for Christmas."

"Christmas be damned! It's too much money. It's money we haven't got." The teakettle started whistling and cut off my father. I heard my mother walk to the stove and shut off the burner.

"Would you like some tea?"

"No. I want you to stop spending money like it's going out of style. I don't break my back at Wagstaff's all day so you can blow the damn money on underwear and nighties."

"I might actually spend the money on lingerie if there was someone here who might appreciate my wearing it. Since you never will, I bought some clothes for Shelley and Jimmy."

"You can't resist the little digs, can you?"

"About as much as you can resist the drunken little lectures." My mother's voice was getting colder and louder at the same time. I could see her in my mind staring at my father across the white surface of the table. I knew, too, that my father would blow up. I just hoped he didn't wake up Jimmy.

"Great." My father's voice took on a new tone. "Here we are having a little talk about the family finances, or lack of them, and she gets uptight. We try to have a little talk about something and she calls it a lecture. That's pretty stupid, you know, and you're supposed to be the one with the brains."

"I don't need your insults."

"No, you got the brains and the money so I can see how you don't need insults, too. How's the dope fiend? Out again?"

"Don't talk like that. Your expectations of her are so low it's no wonder she acts the way she does. She's upstairs writing a letter, I think."

"A letter. Now that's good. Good to have her keep in touch with that unwashed boyfriend. She's turned out real literary, just like you. And she's growing up to look down her nose at me, just like you do. You're teaching her well." My father's voice was getting a crack in it, like some dirt on a record.

"Leave her out of it. You know perfectly well what the problem is—your attitude toward her, and me, and the whole family. You just wallow in this awful self-pity. But do you ever get up the courage to do something for yourself? No. You're a coward. All you can do is drink."

"After busting my ass at work for eight hours, I go out and have a couple of beers. And you say that's the problem. Goddamn. Look. I'll tell you what the problem is. You. It's like Frank says at work, if you're not part of the solution you're part of the problem. He's right. When are you gonna be part of the solution and get a job instead of bleeding my goddamn bank account. You're a leech. I'm married to a leech."

"That's another solution of yours—start calling me names. Well I've got one for you, you coward." I could tell my mother was spitting the words out between her teeth.

On the other side of the bedroom wall I could hear Shelley walking around her room. Jimmy was still asleep. I don't know how he manages to sleep through everything, but it's just as well. I'm older, so I figure I can take the fights better than he can.

"No goddamn leech calls me that. You watch your mouth."

"You are so pathetic. Why don't you just get out of here and go watch the late movie."

"I'll get out of my own kitchen when I damn well feel like it. You don't want me around, go pack up a suitcase. It'll be my parting gift to you. Go bleed somebody else."

"You pathetic coward."

I heard my mother backing toward the refrigerator. She was probably reaching for one of the pans on the wall. My father's chair scraped the floor as he got up and walked toward her.

"Get away from me."

My mother was almost crying now, gasping for breath. She was still trying to control her voice, but starting to break down.

If I were the Hulk, I'd burst into the kitchen and hang each of them on hooks at opposite sides of the room. Or maybe I'd punch my father in the jaw. Or maybe it wouldn't do any good even if I was the Hulk.

There was a crash.

"Oh, God. Oh, merciful God," my mother's voice cried out. Then there was scuffling.

"Get your hands off me."

"Leech, goddamn leech."

"Let go."

I heard the sound of some cloth ripping. There was a second of silence. Then came the worst sound, the way it always ended. My father hit her. For a minute all I could hear was my mother sobbing. Then I heard her run across the floor and the door slam.

She must have gone next door to Mrs. McKirgen's. It was the quiet again downstairs. Shelley's radio wailed. Jimmy slept.

I stayed in bed for about ten minutes after the fight. My heart had started beating really fast, and I got the awful feeling that my knees would collapse if I tried to stand up. I didn't want to go downstairs right away. Besides, when the fight was over I noticed that my cheeks were wet. I didn't want my father to think I'd been crying.

When I felt better I tiptoed down the stairs and looked in the kitchen. My father had buried his head in his arms. His body was very still. He looked up and saw me as I walked in.

"Just going to get some milk," I lied.

"Danny." He reached out his hand to block my path to the refrigerator.

"Yeah."

"Danny," his hand tightened on my arm, "I'm sorry, really." His hand let go and I could see him tighten his muscles, trying not to cry.

"Yeah. It's OK," I lied again. I turned and walked back upstairs. I figured he would have forgotten about the milk anyway.

When I got back to my room, I started thinking about all the other things I could have said. Should have said. They all seemed so useless, like Hulk trying to punch out the interdimensional teleporter.

6

When I got out of the bathroom the next morning, Jimmy had almost as many Cheerios scattered on the table as he had in his bowl.

"Why did you do that?"

"You always say I'm wilted when I have to ask you to make my breakfast," he said, popping the spilled Cheerios into his mouth. He was grinning at me, and it was hard not to grin back.

"Maybe. But you're even more wilted when you spill stuff all over the table."

"Hulk help me clean up? Huh?"

"Hulk say, 'Go chase rolling Cheerio by *self*,'" and I went over to the toaster. Shelley and my mother came into the kitchen together, the one sitting down to coffee, the other putting dishes away.

I kept on trying to look at my mother to see if there were any marks. Sometimes after a fight she really looks beaten up. Two weeks earlier there had been bruises up and down her arms. Shelley kept on saying she should go see somebody. Even senile Dr. Farley would be a start. But no, my mother wouldn't go. She wouldn't even admit to us that he had hit her.

"What are you looking at?" Shelley asked, knowing full well.

"The clock," I lied.

"Oh," Shelley said, drawing out the sound. "I hear you're looking at something else these days."

"What's that supposed to mean?"

"Samantha Morgan."

Now the worst thing you can do when somebody accuses you of being interested in a girl is to turn beet red and get speechless. A little sweat under the armpits is OK, but anything more and you might as well admit the truth. I knew this. So what did I do? I turned beet red and couldn't say a word.

Shelley laughed. "That bad, huh? Hey, Mom . . ."

I didn't wait to hear the rest. My mother turned around and I saw a small bruise on her cheek as I ran out to the hall. My face was so red it felt prickly.

On days like this I make a promise to myself. Whenever I get out of this madhouse I'm going to eat breakfast absolutely alone—no spilled Cheerios, no fights, no smart-ass comments. I figure after twenty years of breakfast grief I'll be due at least twenty years of starting my day even.

Bloop was turning the corner as I raced up the street.

"Nice galoshes," he offered.

"Oh, shut up."

I was probably the only kid in the whole school who still wore rubber boots. The rich kids had nice fake-leather boots like those on Bloop's feet. The poor kids just wore sneakers and pretended they were too tough to care. That's what I would have done, but my mother watched to make sure I didn't "lose" her wonderful boots. Every day I wore these rubber monstrosities and every other day Bloop would make fun of them.

"Touchy this morning . . ." His voice was almost lost in the fur of his parka.

"Yeah. How's the good doctor?" The only way to get back at the Bloop was to make fun of his father, an overweight obstetrician who used to be a Communist before he started making lots of money.

"The good doctor is going bananas, I'm afraid."

"Oh?"

"He started to lecture us on health food while we wolfed potato chips during a movie last night. He's not so crazy that he tries to stop us, you know, but you can start feeling guilty crunching potato chips when somebody's rhapsodizing over wheat germ."

"He's probably just trying to keep your ugly body from falling apart. You eat too much junk food."

"I say," Bloop paused, "there are plenty of fine bodies right in our school that are developing quite well on potato chips and chocolate bars. Like Marilyn Eastman."

"Ooh aah," I yelled while whipping a snowball at a No Parking sign. "Look. Is that Crazy Charlie?"

It was. Off at the Circle, Crazy Charlie was spinning in a circle sending bread crumbs flying to the waiting pigeons. He looked like a perfect madman: long Goodwill coat, two scarves, a hat with earflaps, baggy pants, and rubber boots. He seemed to be having a great time just spinning around like that. In fact,

Charlie always seemed to be having fun. That bothered me. There he was, retarded or schizophrenic or something, and yet he was happy. Why couldn't he be miserable like the rest of us normal people?

On the other hand, chances are that nobody embarrassed him while he was eating breakfast.

"Professor Charles." Bloop waved his hand and Charlie's birds flew away.

"H-hello, students. W-what's new?"

"We were just talking about love and sex, professor. I was wondering if you had any insights that you might be able to give us in that area. Just a word or two. A pearl before us swine."

Crazy Charlie started looking around, as though he was wondering what had happened to his birds. He pulled a dirty handkerchief out of his pocket and wiped his nose.

"Well," he smiled. "Y-you w-want to know about love. This is what I say. Th-this is what I say to all my students at the unifer . . . univers-s-s . . ."

"University," Bloop assisted.

"Yes, at the u-university. I say . . . This is what I say: If you're going to do it, do it right." The face of the idiot philosopher burst into a grin.

"Fantastic, professor, fantastic!" I shouted. "You've done it again. 'If you're going to do it, do it right.' It's genius."

"It's amazing," Bloop joined in with Charlie's favorite word.

"Amazing," Charlie nodded in agreement, "that's right, I'm a-amazing." He bent one arm to make a muscle and looked like an undernourished weight lifter.

"That's really profound. It's the kind of wisdom

they never teach us at school. Thanks so much, professor." The Bloop shook Charlie's hand and we headed off through the snow.

The morning started to look better. There was very little wind, and the snow still hung on the branches giving everything a white outline. The Bloop ran ahead and gave the low branches a shake so the snow would fall on my head. His timing never quite worked.

"I hear that Samantha is going out with Ron Masten," the Bloop said.

"I don't believe it." I could feel a certain coldness in my back when he said it. And I didn't believe it. She'd never go out with somebody as stupid as that. If I wasn't in her league, that guy was so retarded he'd wear a catcher's mitt on his foot.

"That's what Ron said. I told him I thought it was bullshit but he still said it was true. Said they were going to a movie and then fool around at her house. You know."

"Shit."

"I thought you might be interested." Bloop looked at me, looked me right in the eye for at least a second or two. I thought that was pretty strange because we almost never really look at each other.

I didn't say anything more.

"You like her, don't you." Bloop waited for an answer that he didn't get. "Don't ignore me when I ask you a serious question. I may be a wilted, Jewish son-of-a-doctor but I'm also the best friend you've got. Pathetic as that may seem. Now I want the truth. See here shvine . . . ," he started doing his Nazi voice, "ve vill get ze trute out off you if itz ze lazt zing ve do!"

"Yeah."

"Yeah, vat?"

"Yeah, I like her."

"Good," Bloop smiled. "At least you're willing to admit what everybody already knows. That's a sign of mental health, or so my father says. Now ordinarily I wouldn't bug you on such a delicate matter, but I have some additional information you might like."

"Oh?"

"Conzerning ze affections of ze young vench."

"Oh?"

"Well, if you're not interested, never mind." He started skipping off a few steps ahead of me down the sidewalk.

"I'm interested," I said running up to him.

Bloop laughed at me. "All right. Judy Gleason told me yesterday that Sam told her she likes you."

"Really?"

"Would I kid you? You know the only reason she told me was so that I would tell you. Now that you know, the question is when do you make your move?"

"I don't know."

"And what about Ron Masten?"

"I don't know." And I didn't care. The sun had finally made it over the horizon. The sky was that clear blue you can only get on really cold days. The snow started to sparkle on the trees. The cold feeling in my back and the actual cold in my feet and hands disappeared.

" 'I don't know!' Geez. Is that all you can say? We better take you back to the good professor for more philosophy." Bloop laughed and headed through the door into school.

7

I have a bicycle lock on my locker at school. It's against the regulations, but I figured the dollar twenty-five for a school lock would be better spent at McDonald's. My bicycle lock has caused me a lot of problems with Mrs. Edelstein. Her hobby must be memorizing the school regulations. Some teachers can recite Shakespeare, Mrs. Edelstein specializes in the Dress and Behavior Code: "'Each student shall be issued a locker and equip it with an approved combination lock.' That, Danny, is *not* an approved lock."

The lock might have made me seem wilted to the other kids, but I headed that off. I found out, for instance, that the best thing to do when your socks have holes or you can't afford something decent is to pretend that everyone else is out of it. No one wears socks without holes. Everybody knows that perfect socks are wilted. I did the same thing with my lock. When Ron Masten started going bananas over my bike lock, I said, "If you've got three bucks, I'll get one for you." That shut him up. If only I had a line which would do the same to Mrs. Edelstein.

When I got to my locker, there were two people in the hall: Samantha and Mrs. Edelstein. It's not that they made me nervous, but some mornings my combination won't open at first crack. This morning, not even at second crack. Mrs. Edelstein's walking toward me didn't help any.

"Danny," she said, peering over the top of her glasses.

"Yes, ma'am," I said in my innocent voice.

"That lock is not an approved lock."

"Yes, ma'am."

"We can't have five hundred different locks in the school. That one doesn't even fit properly. It seems to me I've spoken to you about this previously. . . ." She stopped with one of those teacher-pauses. With an ordinary human being, you'd know that it was your turn to say something. With a teacher you couldn't be sure. "Yes, I remember distinctly speaking to you about this. When do you expect to do something about it?"

"Forthwith." The big words always throw 'em.

"Forthwith?" She seemed somewhat confused.

"That's right, ma'am." I turned back to my lock. She waited a second and then walked away. It was going to be a good morning.

Sam stood at her locker looking at me. She was beautiful. Blonde hair framed her face perfectly and she had fantastic eyes. Whenever you talked to Sam, those eyes looked up at you as if you were the sexiest person on earth.

Knowing what Judy Gleason had said gave me more courage than usual. On the usual morning, I would have made a goofy face and gotten my books out. This was not a usual morning. I grinned back at her.

"Forthwith?" Sam said. "That's funny."

"Yeah. Teachers are so used to having kids mouth off to them that they don't know what to do when you use some vocabulary. I pick it up from my mother. She's crazy. I think she reads the dictionary before going to bed."

"That beats my mother. The last thing she read was *Reader's Digest*."

"I know. 'Five Hundred Things You Should Know About Today's Teenager,' by Jimmy Carter's great-aunt." I laughed at my own idea and moved a little closer. Another fine thing about Sam which you only noticed close up was her perfume. I like it almost as much as her eyes.

"Uh-hunh. Who's eighty years old and lives with alligators in the middle of . . . there's the warning bell."

"I guess I better get my books," I said.

"Uh-hunh. See you later."

"See you."

Samantha raced off to the homeroom. Mrs. Edelstein stood in the doorway giving us the Frigidaire stare. I watched Sam moving down the hall. There are some other things I like about her besides the eyes and the perfume.

"Danny," Mrs. Edelstein broke in, "are you going to stand there staring all morning?"

"No, sorry." I got my books out and went in for attendance check.

My morning continued going well until lunch. Mrs. Sporbeck, my English teacher, was out, and we had a substitute teacher who looked like Alfred E. Newman.

His face was stretched out sideways so that all you noticed were his apple cheeks and flapping ears. Whenever he stopped watching us, somebody would cough and say "Ears," at the same time. Sort of, "ChchchkEars!" Then he'd look up and frown while you said "Excuse me."

Our cafeteria had been painted some years ago to look like a bowling alley. The walls were colored in terrible browns, pinks, and greens that must have been inspired by the guts of a dissected toad. The ceiling was scarred by the marks of lunchroom battles: streaks of gravy, splotches of chocolate, faint marks of butter. The principal always said that every class left its mark on the school. The ceiling showed he was right.

The Bloop and I had to yell at each other over the noise which went bouncing around the room.

"I saw you talking to Sam this morn . . ." The last part was lost when he bit into his leftover roast-beef sandwich.

"Yeah."

"Well?"

"Well, what?"

"So what happened?" He spit out a piece of bread. "Did you make your move?"

"Not exactly." Now I was embarrassed. How was I supposed to know what to do? I'd never really made any moves before. I mean, it's one thing to ask the prune-faced girl next door to go to a basketball game when you've got an extra ticket, it's something else to come on to Samantha Morgan.

"Geez!" Bloop raised his voice. "Are you wilted! When the girl lets you know she's interested—and she

has—then you're supposed to meet her someplace outside of school and, you know, fool around."

"Where?"

"You can start with her hair and move down or . . ."

"I mean where should I go with her?"

"It doesn't matter. Your house, her house, McDonald's, a movie if you're rich, baby-sitting. Use your
imagination."

So I used my imagination: all through history,
math, and gym. Whenever I get nervous about doing
something, I like to practice in advance. I don't write
down the lines on three-by-cards, that would be
weird, but I play them through in my head. It wasn't
that I was really nervous, it's just that I didn't have
much experience coming on to girls. To be honest, I
didn't have any experience. So I tried out a few lines.
SAM, I WAS WONDERING IF YOU'D LIKE TO
COME OVER TO MY HOUSE AND, YOU KNOW,
FOOL AROUND. No, too obvious. It sounds like the
sort of line Jack the Ripper might use before pulling
out the butcher knife. Try again. SAM, DO YOU
THINK YOU MIGHT WANT TO COME OVER TO
MY HOUSE AND LISTEN TO SOME RECORDS?
Better. there were a few minor problems, though. I'd
have to borrow the stereo from Shelley, who might
give me a hard time. And I didn't have any decent
records. Still, not a bad idea and worth improving.
HEY, SAM, WHY DON'T YOU COME OVER TO
MY PLACE NEXT WEEK AND WE'LL LISTEN TO
RECORDS. That's the line. It sounds so casual that
if she says no I can act as if I were just asking her for
a homework assignment. If you're going to get shot
down, there's no sense going down in flames.

At the end of the last class, I raced back to my locker so I wouldn't miss her. I had to shuffle through some notebooks for several centuries until she got to her locker. Except for my legs, which were sort of weak, I was ready to deliver the line. No stalling. I walked over to her locker.

"Hi, Danny."

"Hey, Sam . . ."

"Uh-hunh."

"Well, I was thinking, maybe. You know, maybe we should . . . uh."

"That'd be great. Why don't you come over to my house after school on Monday?"

"Sure. Great. See you then."

Like I said, rehearsing the line helps my confidence a lot.

▓▓

8

Nobody ever has two good days in a row. That's what Bloop says and he has the luck. When Bloop finds something lying in the street, it's a guy's wallet with five bucks inside and no ID to make him feel guilty. Whenever I find something, it turns out to be somebody's left-hand glove with holes in two fingers and mold on the lining. Some people have the luck, some don't. But even people who have it don't have two good days in a row.

On Friday, what little luck I did have took off as if it suddenly discovered I had leprosy. Friday should have been a good day. The teachers had one of their conferences and the schools were closed to give us a long weekend. My father was on the day shift, so he wouldn't be around to bug us. My mother was acting more human lately and less like the warden of a German concentration camp. When I woke up, the sun was shining.

I could hear my mother downstairs talking to some

man I didn't know. I caught a certain edge on her voice that meant trouble so I threw on my jeans and hurried downstairs. What could be more heroic, I thought, than saving my mother from escaped bank robbers. Sometimes I think the chance to be heroic justifies the other three hundred sixty-four days of the year when you go about your average, wilted life.

When I got downstairs I was disappointed. No bank robbers. Not even vandals or pickpockets. One overweight man stood by the basement door dressed in white overalls. He carried a clipboard with pink and green forms on it and was marked by a label on his chest as a serviceman from Robinson's. He had a kid with him, not much older than I am. The kid looked really dirty compared to the old guy in white. I guess the kid had to do all the work and didn't even rate a pair of overalls.

"Look, lady," the old guy was saying, "I just got this order slip which says the washer got to go back. I don't know nothing about payments or the credit department. You know, I just do a job."

The kid was rubbing his nose. He looked pretty bored. My mother, on the other hand, seemed full of energy, as if she had been expecting some sort of showdown all week.

"Are you certain there's no mistake? That's all I'm trying to find out."

"Your name Morrison?"

"Yes."

"This 232 Spadina?"

"Yes. But this paper really doesn't tell you anything, or give you any right . . ."

"Lady, the order form says take the washer back. I

don't know about rights and lefts. I ain't a lawyer. I just gotta move the washer. *You* gotta problem, *you* call Customer Service, the number's right there."

He went down to the basement and left my mother standing at the top of the stairs holding on to a pink paper with a telephone number.

"What's going on?" I said, not because I didn't know but because I thought I should say something.

"Your father missed too many payments on the washer. They're taking it back."

"Geez."

"There's no reason to swear, Danny. Your father chooses to spend his money on other things, like drinking at the local tavern, so what else can you expect?"

She paused after the word "tavern" for emphasis. I kept on thinking I should do something. My reading Hulk comics didn't help much. Can you imagine a serviceman coming to take away Hulk's washing machin? "Hulk say check is *in* mail, no take away washer." Pretty dumb.

My mother went out to the kitchen and sat down. Jimmy came running downstairs to see the excitement. The two men from Robinson's came up from the basement with the washer. The kid had straps around his shoulders and was lifting the weight pretty much by himself. They got it out to the truck and came back for some hoses. At the door, old Overalls tried to be nice.

"Sorry about this, Miz Morrison. These things happen."

"Yeah, especially if you don't pay your bills," the kid cut in.

By the time I figured out that I should have slugged the kid, he was already out the door. Some nerve. The kid stands around wiping his nose with a finger and then insults us as he leaves. I felt the muscles in my arms tighten but there was nothing to swing at. I looked over at my mother. She sat at the table rubbing her hands as if she were putting lotion on them. But there wasn't any lotion.

"You OK, Mom?"

"How much longer are we going to put up with this?"

"Huh?"

"How much degradation am I expected to take from these . . . these idiots. And you know who's at fault, don't you? Yes, you know. I can put up with hardship. Lord knows, I have put up with hardship for seventeen years. But when he subjects me to degradation . . . there are limits. There are limits."

She was quiet. I didn't know what to say so I decided to shut up. She went to make coffee and I went back upstairs.

I knew there was going to be some kind of trouble when my father came home. My mother could really hold a grudge and nurse it. I remember once she did a real number on my father when we were driving to the beach. She said she was just paying him back for insulting her at a party two years earlier. Two years. Imagine remembering something like that for two years. They say that Mrs. Edelstein and Dr. Clow at school haven't spoken to each other for thirteen years over some problem nobody else can remember. I guess you have to be an adult to be ready for really long-term anger. That's what I've got to look forward to.

When you know trouble is coming, it gives you a kind of funny excitement. You know whatever happens you're going to come out a loser, so the only real question is whether you want to watch it happen or let it sneak up on you. Do you take the handkerchief or watch the bullets come at you? I decided to watch. I talked to Shelley and she took Jimmy out so he wouldn't have to be around. She thought I should stay in case Mom got hurt.

My mother was out in the kitchen when my father came in the back door. I couldn't see directly, but the dining-room mirror reflected most of the room. That way I could watch without having my body in the path of flying dishes.

"They took the washer away," my mother said, smiling, looking almost proud.

"Wha?" My father had been drinking.

"The men from Robinson's came and took the washer away. One of them insulted me before he left."

"The bastards."

"Always blaming somebody else, aren't you. No, the problem is not with some serviceman and his manners. It's not with the store. The problem is you. You. Why can't you face up to it?"

"Look, let's not get angry about this, huh?" My father looked like a kid. In his half-drunk state he was no match for my mother. I felt sorry for him. He slumped down at the table, resting his forehead against the palm of his hand. My mother was over at the stove, still smiling.

"I am not angry. I am speaking with absolute clarity. If you weren't soused you could see that. This morning I saw our situation with amazing clarity. You call me a leech. You're wrong. You're the drain on the family, on our love and our money. And you should get out. We don't need you."

"Wha?"

"Get out. We can make it without you. Send me what you can for the kids. We'll get by. And I won't have to listen to your insults or your bullying. You know why you hit me? Because you're weak. Because you're afraid of everything else out there, afraid of what they'll do to you. You're not afraid of me because I've put up with your filthy habits for seventeen years. Well, I don't have to anymore. I won't."

"Sue, now wait a minute."

"Yes, I'll wait. But you think about what I've said. You think I'm a leech, you'll see. Take a day to think about it. But either you straighten your life around or you get out."

I was scared. I rarely saw my mother like this, sure of herself and strong.

"You think you're such a bloody hell. Maybe you'll see. Maybe I really will go. Huh? How'd you like that? Think you can do it all by yourself. We'll see." My father got up and started moving up the stairs.

"You choose. You choose what's important to you," my mother was still cool, "but we can take care of ourselves."

I felt cold, sitting out in the living room. There were goose bumps on my arms. My parents had often threatened to separate in the past. Sometimes one or the other would go off to a relative for a day or so. But they always came back together with an awful scene full of tears and hugging. This time it seemed different. My mother's voice was so cold and so serious. If she had been yelling and angry it wouldn't have been so bad. But she seemed to know precisely what she was saying. How could either of them explain it away tomorrow?

I went over and sat on the radiator. Upstairs I could hear my father in the bathroom. He was throwing up.

9

On Monday morning, breakfast was pretty quiet. My mother padded around in her slippers like some creature that had fallen into a swamp and come out like a blob instead of the Hulk. My sister looked strung out. They were both nervous. I was nervous, too, about something else.

Nobody said anything. While I was putting jelly on my toast, Shelley leaned over in my direction and sniffed. She must have figured out that I was wearing the Old Spice cologne my father got for Christmas last year. She looked at me for a second and seemed about to say something. Then she turned back to her coffee.

Thank God. If Shelley and my mother were less caught up in their own problems they would have known I was up to something from the amount of time I spent in the bathroom. Ordinarily, two minutes of splashing has me set for the day. Today, I showered, brushed my hair, sprayed my pits at least ten seconds a side, and even used dental floss. When I

came out of the bathroom, the cloud of steam brought
a deadly concentration of Right Guard and Old Spice.
Any insects flying by would have fallen dead in mid-
air.

I left for school a little late. I thought I'd start the
day without Bloop's wisecracks and Charlie's philosophy. There wasn't too much snow on the ground and
that was a break. I just couldn't wear those wilted
rubber boots while walking Samantha home.

I made it through the day without seeming too nervous, I think. Last period I asked Mrs. Sporbeck if I
could go to the bathroom and—this was my second
break—she didn't give me a hard time. When I entered
the washroom, the smokers in the far stalls waited a
second to check my footsteps and then kept puffing
away. They couldn't see me at the mirror, so I got out
my brush and went to work on my hair. I took a couple of peppermint Life Savers out of my shirt pocket,
chewed them so quickly they made me sneeze, and
checked my breath. Huhhh. OK. I had taken care of
most of the blackheads the night before. That left
only the pimple on my cheek which always fattened
up when I got nervous and a brand-new one near my
ear which really hurt but I couldn't get at it. I saw
that my shirt was wet under the armpits. Guess I
didn't use enough Right Guard. I took a look at myself: fair, maybe even OK. The glasses didn't help
much but didn't make me look too wilted, either. I
started testing a few faces in the mirror when another
kid came through the door. I froze the expression on
my face and headed back to class.

Samantha was waiting at her locker when I got to
mine. She looked great. The wisps of blond hair
caught the light in the corridor and made it play with

shimmers and sparkles. She was wearing a white shirt and jeans which clung tightly to her: a little skinny, but nice.

I felt funny looking at her. I couldn't figure out why she'd be interested in me. Why not one of the upperclassmen, or Fred Mihalowicz on the football team, or even the Bloop? It just didn't make sense. Me? At the same time, I felt proud. Sam was waiting for me to take her home. I wanted to shout it down the halls, hey, she's waiting for me. I wanted to show off to all the people who thought I wasn't important: my father, Shelley, Ron Masten, Mrs. Edelstein. Look, you idiots, this girl is waiting for me to take her home. Now, that's a nice feeling.

"Are you ready?" she said, putting her coat on. It was a light-brown coat that looked like it cost a couple hundred dollars. My parka was pretty ratty in comparison.

"Just a second." I wondered if I should carry her books home. How embarrassing. What if she's liberated and tells me to screw off? I decided to use a compromise line, "You want to add your books to my pile?"

"Sure."

We walked to the door. I'm certain the eyes of everyone in the hall were on us. That made me feel good. It also made me feel nervous. You never realize how awkward you walk until you know people are watching you.

We talked mainly about school on the way to her house. I figured I was doing pretty well. There were two good signs: she seemed to laugh a lot at what I said and she bumped into me three, no, four times while we walked on the slippery sidewalks. This could mean that she liked me. On the other hand, it might only mean that she laughs easy and the sidewalk's slippery. That's the trouble with girls. You never know when they're giving you some kind of message and when they're just being normal.

"My mother is going to descend on you when we get in," she said as we got to her corner.

"Oh?"

"Don't get too upset with her. She's like that all the time. Dad says she can't help it. She goes away pretty quick if you're nice to her."

"Sure I'll be nice. See the nice-guy smile." I smiled like an Ultra Brite model. It made her laugh.

Sam unlocked the door to her house. The door had a bronze knocker, a little hand-operated bell, and an electric bell switch with a light. The hardware alone was worth more than my whole front porch.

Sam's mother descended while she was hanging our coats in the closet. I saw why she used the word descended. Her mother was a big woman, taller than me and weighing a good two hundred pounds. The woman moved down the hall at you as if she were a linebacker for the Green Bay Packers. I faded back into the wall and knocked over the umbrella stand.

"Oh, I'm sorry."

"No, it's my fault. I didn't mean to startle you. You must be Jimmy."

"Uh . . . no, Danny."

"Oh, Danny. That's right. Well, I'm *so* glad you're here. Would you like some tea after you tour the house?"

I didn't know what to say. I looked over to Sam for help. She made a little movement with her head to say no. "Thanks very much, Mrs. Morgan, but we were just going to do some homework and really don't need any."

"Oh, I see. Well, Sam will take you around the house, and if you need anything, just let me know." She padded off.

Sam looked at me as if to say, I warned you. What she really said was, "You don't want a house tour, do you?"

"No."

"My mother forces everybody to tour the house and see her antiques," she whispered. "I think it's part of change of life."

"Yeah," I said, not sure what she meant. The house was fantastic. The furniture all looked like it was hundreds of years old. God forbid anybody should actually sit on it or spill a Coke. The house looked great, but I didn't know how anybody could live in it. Sam led me along the hall down into the rec room. I breathed a little easier. There was a fake fireplace at one end, a folded-up Ping-Pong table in the corner, some old chairs and a couch, a padded bar, an ironing board, and even some dirt on the shag rug.

"This is where we actually live," Sam said. "The upstairs is for my mother and her friends." She went over and sat on the couch.

This gave me a problem. To sit next to her on the couch might be a little too fast. I'd also have to figure out how far away from her I should stay. But if I sat across from her in a chair, she might think I wasn't really interested in her and just came to play records. I stalled by walking over to the stereo. "What do you want to hear?" I asked.

"Wait a minute. If she's on time today, my mother will be down to check on you and embarrass me in about ten seconds."

I counted. At nine seconds, Mrs. Morgan came down the stairs. "Danny," she called in a high pitched voice, "did you know that Sam is a very accomplished organist?"

"No, really?"

"Yes, she's been taking lessons for two years. . . ."

"A little over a year, Mother," Sam cut in.

"Almost two years," Mrs. Morgan couldn't be stopped, "and everybody thinks she's just marvelous. Wouldn't you like her to play something for you?"

Sam was saying no, no with little shakes of her head. But Mrs. Morgan was gesturing like a grizzly bear standing on its hind legs. I figured I'd risk Sam rather than the bear.

"Sure."

"Oh, God, Mother!" Sam wasn't happy.

"Come on, now. Everyone enjoys your playing. Do a song by Frank Sinatra for me. 'My Way.' The music's right there. Do you like Frank Sinatra, Danny?"

"Uh."

"Here. It's warmed up for you, Sam. Now play."

Samantha moved over to the organ like a condemned prisoner. I felt sorry for her. She shuffled the music on the rack and started playing "Love Me Tender," one of the songs Elvis Presley used to sing. She was great. Her hands zipped over the keyboard, pressing notes and flipping levers. Mrs. Morgan looked like she was in another world. I guess she wasn't all that set on Frank Sinatra herself.

When Sam was finished, Mrs. Morgan started applauding, so I did too. Sam frowned at her mother but she gave me a different look.

"If you don't *mind*, Mother, we have some studying to do."

"Of course, of course. I just *knew* that Danny would want to hear you play. Wasn't she marvelous, Danny? Wouldn't you like some tea? Are you sure?" Mrs. Morgan hit me with three questions at once.

Rather than say yes, no, yes, I offered, "Thanks, we're fine."

Her grizzly-bear shape went up the stairs. I breathed more easily. Sam flopped down on the couch. She started laughing.

"She's such a cartoon," Sam whispered, "sometimes I can't stand it."

"She just likes showing you off. You're the star."

"I'm the last star left. My two sisters got out when they went to college and haven't come back. Once Johanna pretended to go to Florida over Christmas and just stayed in her dorm to avoid coming home. The worst thing about my mother is that she's so predictable. She's gone now but she'll be back in ten minutes on some excuse. Clockwork."

"I guess we better start doing some homework," I said, somewhat relieved. Under circumstances like these I really couldn't do anything. I mean, how could I come on with the grizzly overhead?

"Uh-hunh. I'll put on this new album and we can start the history assignment."

Sam put on K-Tel's latest, medium loud. She got out her history book which was a lot like our history teacher: ancient. Sam was better at history than I was. It's not that I'm dumb, but who really cares about the depth of the St. Lawrence Seaway? And when the book starts talking about "tertiary causes of the War of 1812," all I can do is wonder how a turtle could start a war.

Sam's mother was a little late. We could hear her walking on the floor overhead before she came down. Sam gave me a look.

"Sorry to bother you. I just had to check a piece of furniture out in this price book. Is your house done in antiques, Danny?"

"Not exactly," I said. Half my house looked like it came directly from the Salvation Army and the other half was probably bought with Green Stamps. Still, you could sit on the furniture without worrying whether your jeans were dirty.

Mrs. Morgan flipped through some pages in a book, seemed to find something, and went upstairs. Sam and I pretended to be writing. Actually, we were looking at each other trying hard not to laugh.

"Clockwork," I said.

"Uh-hunh. Hey, do you want some eggnog? My mother makes it with six million eggs and tons of cream."

"Sounds great. After I have some I can model for a Clearasil ad. The 'Before' part."

Sam laughed and ran upstairs to the refrigerator. A minute later she came down with a pitcher and a couple of glasses. She put the eggnog down on the coffee table in front of the couch and sat down. I joined her and drank some.

"Wow."

"Didn't I say it had rum in it?" Sam's teeth sparkle when she smiles.

"It's great. I love the whipped cream floating on top. All *we* ever get is eggnog from the store." I don't know if it was the drink, or the room, or Sam, but I started feeling a little warm.

"You've got a mustache."

"No, I shaved this morning."

"Not that kind of mustache, dummy. There's whipped cream on your lip. There's even some on your nose."

I made a big show about licking away my mustache, even crossing my eyes to make Sam laugh.

"You missed some."

"Where?"

"Here." Sam reached forward and touched the corner of my mouth with her finger. I kept on looking at her. We were both quiet for a second.

"You've got a mustache, too," I said.

"Where?"

"Here."

I leaned forward and kissed her, forgetting that I was nervous, forgetting that I didn't know how. Her lips were perfectly soft. We stopped. She opened her eyes and then closed them. We kissed again. This time she opened her mouth a little and I could feel her tongue touch my lips. Her hand went around my shoulder to where the feeling of electricity was running up and down my back. I touched her tongue with mine.

We were together for some time. I don't know how long. The record came to its end on the stereo and started clicking over the speakers. We never did finish the history homework.

Sam's mother started walking on the floor overhead. I pulled back from Sam on the couch. She smoothed her hair a bit and coughed. Her mother plodded down the stairs.

"Oh. Samantha, I just wanted to say that we're having dinner in about twenty minutes. Would Danny want to stay for dinner?"

She looked at me. I wanted to stay, but I couldn't. "I'm sorry, Mrs. Morgan, but I have to baby-sit my little brother tonight. Maybe some other time."

"Well, you're always welcome. Did you get your homework done?"

"Yes, we got quite a bit done." I think I was blushing when I said this, so I got up to hide my embarrassment.

A minute later Sam stood with me in the doorway. I got my coat on and walked to the front step. She pulled the door mostly closed behind her.

"Thanks," I said.

"Uh-hunh," she said. I kept on looking at her eyes. They caught the light even in the darkness of the street. "Here's one to take home with you." She put a kiss on her fingertip and touched my lips.

"See you."

10

The morning was fantastic. The sun had just come up and was casting long shadows when its light hit a house or a tree. The icicle outside my bedroom window trapped the morning light inside it and glowed. I opened the window to let the air in, cold and fresh.

Jimmy woke up. "Hey, you're freezing me out."

"Wake up, you idiot. The air will do you good." I grinned at him. My body felt hot from sleeping in the overheated room.

"You're crazy."

"You're right." I went over, got my pillow, and threw it at him. "I'm crazy. I'm tired of being normal. Normal is boring. I want to be crazy."

I had a strange kind of energy running through me. When I looked around the room I noticed things I hadn't seen for years. Parts of the Erector set under the radiator. Jimmy's cuddly bear in the closet with the stuffing coming out. My piles of comic books in

the corner. I saw their shapes and colors as if I had
been on a long trip and just come back.

"It's magic," Jimmy said.

"What?"

"Magic. One day you're dull, the next day you're
crazy." He yawned and started to get dressed.

"And I'm gonna stay crazy."

"Forever?"

"Yeah, forever."

I couldn't face breakfast with my family, so I swal-
lowed a cup of coffee in two gulps and left. Jimmy
could get his own Cheerios now, anyway.

The air outside was perfectly crisp and it made my
nose and cheeks tingle. I watched my breath turn into
steam for a while and then tried to do some tricks. I
blew short puffs, long streams, sent Morse code mes-
sages in frozen air. I felt light as if the guys who make
gravity had gone on strike. I skidded across the slippery sidewalk and punched holes in the fragile sec-
tions of ice that look like crystals.

I was aware of my body. The clunky parts of it that
had hung together for fourteen years now seemed
beautiful. My lips were soft and sensitive. I could
bring back the feeling of Samantha's kiss just by
touching my lips with my glove.

My imagination worked overtime. Sam was with
me . . . next to me . . . kissing . . .

"What are you grinning about?"

It was the Bloop. He had been standing right in
front of me and I hadn't even seen him. In fact, I
really didn't want to see him. He spoiled some of the
magic of the day.

"Well, look," he said noticing my frown, "if you
really don't want me around I'll disappear."

"No, it's OK," I lied. "I was just thinking about a few things."

"Give me three guesses: the state of Chinese-Russian relations. Wrong. The theory of relativity. Wrong. Samantha Morgan. Oh, oh. I can tell by your skin color that I've hit it dead on."

"Geez, how'd you know?"

"Judy Gleason. She's got the biggest mouth in school. While you were home last night staring at the moon and dreaming of escape to the nearest star, Sam was talking to Judy on the phone." Bloop's version came complete with a pantomime, so I had to laugh.

"Actually, I was dreaming that Sam and I were on a boat."

"Oh, really?" Bloop shifted into his German psychiatrist accent. "Zat ist very zexual, you know. Ist full of hidden zignificance. Yah?"

"Really?"

"How should I know? Isn't everything you dream about supposed to be sexual. I mean, if you were dreaming about Samantha and it wasn't sexual, maybe you need some help. Some professional help. Now my father's office hours . . ."

I threw a snowball at him to shut him up. Then I took off down the street before he could make one to throw back. I knew the Bloop would never run to catch up with me.

"I hear you did all right," he yelled.

"None of your business," I yelled back.

"Oh, yeah? I've still got some information you need."

I was tempted to run off further and leave him. But Bloop had a way of getting information which was useful. Without that clue from Judy Gleason, I'd be no

closer to Sam than staring at the back of her head in
math class. I decided to wait for Bloop to catch up.

"What is it?"

"You may have a problem." His voice got serious.

"With Sam?"

"No, with Ron Masten. I imagine that everyone in
school will know that you two are going together.
Ron's not going to like it. He's been after Sam all year,
you know."

"So what?"

"So nothing. I'm just telling you to be cautious.
Ron's really an animal in a lot of ways. He's primitive
and therefore unpredictable. He may do nothing, in
which case you've got nothing to worry about. But he
may decide to do something and he's so crazy I can't
predict what it's going to be."

I didn't know what to say. I used to pretend that I
was a tough kid. That was easy in elementary school.
But lately I'd been thinking that the tough-kid act was
pretty dumb, if not dangerous. I remember in history
class Mrs. Jennings gave us what she called a moral
dilemma. Suppose you were walking down the street
and saw three kids beating up an old man, what
would you do? I put up my hand with everybody else
when she said, "Who would go in and help the old
man?" but I was lying. I knew that I'd probably just
run to telephone the police so I wouldn't have to get
involved. Or when that appliance serviceman insulted
my mother, I didn't have to let him out the door. I
knew what he meant and what I should do while he
was still in the hall. But I waited the extra couple of
seconds so I wouldn't have to get involved. Maybe
that's being a coward or maybe it's figuring out that

one punch won't solve anything important. Still, I couldn't back down to Ron Masten. Even a coward can draw a line. I drew mine around Samantha and me. He had lots of room to move outside the line. If he forced his way inside . . . I didn't know what I'd do.

"And let me do you a favor," Bloop added. "If Ron tries something, don't rely on your feeble brain for a response. Talk to me first, huh?"

"Sure."

That was good advice. Bloop always gave good advice. He never got involved in fights. He once said, "If I'm going to get in a fight, it's not going to be a kindergarten shoving match, it's going to be a real fight. I'll try to put the kid out quick and for good. I'll get him in the crotch, in the eyes, and in the neck." He meant it, too. Nobody ever pushed him into a fight because it wasn't a game for him, it was serious business. Most of the bullies in school weren't up to serious business.

When we got near my locker, I saw Sam across the way. I left Bloop without saying anything. When Sam smiled at me from across the hall I really didn't see anything but her. It's like being in a play when the lights suddenly go out on stage and there's a spotlight on one person. There was Sam, in my spotlight.

"Hi."

"Hi."

"Did you get your history finished?" She laughed.

"Oh, shit. I knew I was supposed to do something last night."

"Here, I'll give you mine." She took the paper out of

her notebook. "You can copy it over during study hall."

"Thanks. You want to come over to my place after school?"

"Sure."

"The house isn't very nice, you know. But I can guarantee that my mother will be out. It'll just be you, me, and my wilted little brother."

"How old is he?"

"Seven going on two. He just got out of diapers last year. I tell him he's brain damaged."

"Great." She looked at me. "You know what . . ." She just kept on looking at me, that was the "what." "Uh-oh, Mrs. Edelstein's staring at us."

I looked over at the room and there was Mrs. Edelstein. Smiling. What a way to start the day.

I felt nervous walking home with Sam. I thought I knew where I stood with her, but I wasn't sure. It could be I was just another friend and she was a naturally friendly person. Or maybe the other day she had suffered temporary insanity and today she'd come back to normal. Or maybe she was just teasing me along to make somebody else jealous. We didn't say much to each other walking to my house, and these thoughts kept coming back to me.

My house looked pretty awful when we came up to it. I felt like I was seeing it with new eyes. The wooden porch sagged a bit, the concrete steps had big cracks, two of the plastic storm windows had split open in the wind and made a flapping sound. I thought I should apologize to Sam for the house being cruddy so I turned to her. She looked at me as if to say, "It's OK," so I shut up. Maybe she didn't care.

We got inside and shook the snow off.

"Your nose is red. So are your ears." Her fingers touched after her words.

"Yeah. I should buy one of those masks that skiers wear."

"A balaclava?" she said.

"Anything you say, I'm easy," I laughed. "Well, in the words of your mother, would you like to see the house?"

"Uh-hunh."

"It's a very quick tour 'cause it's a very small house. On this floor we have the kitchen where my mother breaks the dishes after my father threatens to strangle her. And here's the living room where they make up the next day. Note the baby shoes in the corner shelf, they're mine."

"I bet you were cute."

"I had very nice toes. Everyone thought I had great toes. That's why they only kept the shoes, the rest of my body was wilted. Now the dining-room suite is currently out for refinishing, like it's been out for the last twenty years, so we usually eat in the kitchen. That blob on the kitchen floor is where my brother Jimmy always spills his Cheerios. It's turned into a permanent part of the house: a fossil of petrified Cheerios. And the staircase leads upstairs to the bedrooms. . . ."

I started to go up the stairs but could feel Sam hold back. Instead of standing beside me she was two steps behind me and not smiling. There was a different look in her eyes.

"No. I know what you're thinking but I'm not a rapist or anything. I mean, Jimmy will be home in five minutes anyhow."

"And bedrooms are all alike," she added.

"Yeah, I was just gonna say that. Bedrooms are all alike so we don't have to see them. Besides, the smell would knock you dead."

"Smell?"

"Incense. My sister burns it whenever she smokes dope. It's been gradually leaking out of her room so now the whole floor smells. Hey, you wanna eat?"

We plowed through the refrigerator and found some salami and mustard. I ran up to my room and got the Coke I keep next to the window so it will stay cold. When I got downstairs, Jimmy had already come in.

"Are you Jimmy?" Sam asked.

"Yeah. You must be Samantha. You know, Danny's in love with you. Can I have a salami sandwich too?"

I think I would have smashed the kid if he hadn't looked so small climbing out of his leggings. Little brothers are supposed to be a pain, and I can live with that, but do I have to put up with embarrassment too?

"Sure." Samantha smiled at him.

"Look, Jimmy, why don't you go upstairs and play?" I said.

"I just got here."

"You got here two minutes ago and already you bother me. Go upstairs and pretend you know how to read."

"After I eat my sandwich." He took a bite and then added with his mouth full, "And only if you play Hulk tonight."

"Deal," I said.

"Deal," he said, shaking my hand and spitting out a bit of bread. What a slob!

It actually took a while longer to get rid of Jimmy. He kept on hanging around for one reason or another. Even after he went to our bedroom he kept on coming back down. He said he had to feed the goldfish. As if the goldfish wasn't perfectly happy to wait an hour or two.

Sam found our family album out on the lamp table. I guess my mother had been going through it the night before and left it. That was pretty unusual because she didn't really trust us with it. Sam and I snuggled together on the couch.

"Who's the guy with the bow tie?"

"That's my uncle Phil," I said, sliding my arm around her. "He invented a wonder drug and made a fortune. Then he lost it all by investing in bowling alleys. Last time anybody saw him, he was paddling a canoe up the Gatineau River."

"Is he crazy?"

"My whole family on my mother's side is crazy. My uncle Bill used to be in prison in Argentina. My aunt Doris is president of a croquet club in Arizona."

"They must play on sand dunes."

"I don't know where they play, but she says it's a good excuse to drink a lot of Coors. She's the exact opposite of my mother, who never drinks anything harder than orange juice."

"Is this your mother getting married?"

"Yeah, you can't see that she's pregnant, can you?"

"Pregnant?"

"Yeah, with my sister Shelley. We found their marriage certificate once and figured it out. She must have been four months pregnant. That's why they never celebrate their anniversary."

"This must be you."

"As a baby." I got closer to smell the perfume.

"What a cute mouth you had."

"Still do," I said, getting closer.

"That's a pretty vain thing to say."

"Only if I'm lying. Try it."

She did.

11

That night my father came home from work for the last time. It's hard to describe clearly what happened. It's not that I don't remember it clearly or that it wasn't clear at the time. It's like describing a nightmare the day after. All the things that had been so perfectly clear and perfectly terrifying seem to lose their shape the next day.

I was sitting on the couch looking at the paper to see what movies were playing. Jimmy and Shelley were at the table in the dining room playing Chinese checkers. My mother was ironing in the kitchen.

My father came in without saying anything and headed up the stairs. He often came in without talking to the rest of us and maybe it was better that way. Shelley made a move on the checkerboard that must have taken her from one end to the other, I heard so many jumps. My mother's iron hissed out in the kitchen. There were clunking sounds from upstairs.

The rest was like a silent movie. We all kept on doing what we were doing and no one said a word. One by one we figured out what my father was doing: packing.

I think I was the first to figure it out. There was something about the sound of doors opening and drawers sliding that didn't make any sense, or made sense only if he was actually leaving. When I figured it out, I was looking at an ad for a science-fiction movie. Even though I was wearing my glasses, I couldn't seem to focus on the ad.

When I turned to look at Shelley, I could see that she knew what was happening, too. She had stopped playing Chinese checkers and her eyes were looking ahead at nothing. Jimmy was staring at her, impatient.

In the kitchen, the iron hissed.

It was quiet for an awfully long time. I don't think Jimmy noticed anything, but it was unusual for him to be quiet for as long as he was. I thought of saying something to Shelley, but didn't know what. We all seemed frozen into our positions by the silence.

My father came down the stairs with a couple of our old suitcases. The three of us watched him. Jimmy figured it out, I think, but didn't say anything.

My father looked very old as he put the bags down. You never really look at people in your family except at certain special moments. This was a moment for a long look. My father was lost. He was like a little kid set to run away from home, pretty sure why, but really scared as to how he's going to do it. My father's eyes kept moving around. He wouldn't really look at us or the house or anything. At one point he opened his mouth as if he was going to say something to us.

But all that came out was a rush of air, and then the silence came back. He picked up the bags and went out the door.

My vision was pretty blurred by this time. Shelley took Jimmy upstairs and they started talking as they went. I went out to the kitchen to see how my mother was. She stood there staring. I don't think she knew I was in the room. She looked all right, sort of stiff, but all right. I turned and left her. The only sound was the hissing of the iron.

Jimmy was in his bed crying when I got up to the room. He had pulled his covers up over his eyes and his feet stuck out. He looked like a bird that had been run over by a car.

"Hey, come on," I said. "What's the big deal. You gotta toughen up a little bit, you know."

"Daddy's gone," he wailed.

"Oh, Daddy's mad all right. But he'll be back. You know how they are when they get mad."

"You think so?"

"Sure," I lied. "Now stop the crying. You're starting to get *me* upset."

"Shelley says he's gone for good."

"What does she know?"

"She's older than you."

"Look, I tell you it's all right. He'll be back. Now stop acting like a baby. Get these covers off. I'm tired of talking to a ball of blankets."

Jimmy pulled the blankets off. I handed him some Kleenex I kept by the bed. He blew his nose and stuck the paper under the mattress while I shook my head. His nose and eyes were all red and his hair had been mashed by the blankets.

"Danny?"

"Huh."

"How come you're so tough."

"Not me. I gave up fighting a couple years ago."

"I don't mean that. I mean nothing ever bothers you."

"Oh, lots bothers me. You think I'm not bothered when Mom and Dad fight? No, you're wrong. I just hold it in. It always blows over sooner or later. And it doesn't do any good for me to cry, or fight, or stick my nose in. You learn that kind of thing when you get older."

"I wish I was older."

"Just hang in there."

Jimmy started crying again for no reason that I could figure out. I mean, it wasn't anything I said. He just started sniffling and then really crying. His body folded forward into a ball and I couldn't think of anything to say, so I held him. His body heaved in my arms. When he was done, he fell back on the bed.

"Sorry," he said, grabbing more Kleenex.

"It's OK."

"I feel awful. Like I wanna throw up."

"Don't. I'd rather have you cry. Listen, I told you earlier that I'd be Hulk. Would you like that?"

"Yeah." Some life came back to his voice. "Sit back here."

I sat back against the end of the bed and Jimmy settled into the nook of my arm.

"Here's the story. It was a quiet night in the swamp. The bullfrogs were going brr-ook brr-ook but otherwise it was strangely quiet. The alligators were all asleep."

"Alligators don't sleep," Jimmy broke in.

"Sure they do. And it's my story so the alligators are all asleep. Even the Hulk is resting. A car drives up to the edge of the swamp and its lights shine over the ooze. A man gets out of the car and throws two packages into the water. In the front seat is a woman. She's crying. The motor of the car starts and it pulls away. Rrrrum. Rrrrum. The Hulk hears the noises and gets suspicious. He rises out of the ooze and dead leaves and goes over to where the car had been. He sees the two packages. One is still moving. Hulk thinks, 'This not full of *junk*. This is *alive*. Lucky I got here, otherwise the chemical in the swamp ooze would turn these into . . . into Hulks like me.' The Hulk pulls off the string and finds two boys inside, half alive."

"String?"

"Yeah, the kids were drugged at dinner and tied up when they were unconscious, so they didn't need rope. Now the Hulk is thinking, 'I will *nurse* these two back to health and *save* them. They will not turn like me into . . . into *Hulk*.' It takes a long time to bring the kids back to health. Hulk has to feed them berries and bananas from the swamp."

"Bananas?"

"Well, maybe not bananas. But he brings the two kids back to health. The Hulk says, 'Why those two *people* want to kill you?' And the little kid says, 'Because that man is our stepfather and he didn't want us. He forced our mother to go along and then tried to kill us.' Hulk says, 'They say that *I* am not human, but I am *too human* to do that. *I* will protect you.' "

I could tell by Jimmy's weight that he was asleep. I guess he wasn't all that interested in the Hulk's revenge. The story was getting dumb, anyhow. I pulled

my arm from in back of his neck and settled him
down in his bed.

I wasn't very sleepy. Shelley was playing her radio
and smoking dope. Where was Mangy Bob when she
needed him?

I creaked down the stairs to get something to eat
from the kitchen. In the living room I could see my
mother lying on the couch. She was asleep. I went a
little closer. On the floor was our old family album.
She must have been looking at it before she fell
asleep. Some of the pages had gotten bent when it fell
so I tried to straighten them out before laying the
whole book flat on the floor.

I poured myself some milk in the kitchen because
there wasn't anything to eat and my stomach didn't
feel very good. I was cold. After a while my breathing
started to come a little funny and I knew I was crying.
I said to myself that I should stop it, that the Hulk
wouldn't cry. But I knew that that was only because
the Hulk wasn't real.

I laid my head in my arms and sobbed. I guess it
was my turn.

12

When I woke up the next morning I was squeezing the life out of the balled-up blanket in my grip. The room was hot and I was sweaty. My clock read a quarter to seven which really meant it was six-thirty. I always set it fast so I can fool myself into waking up early. I think this year maybe I should stop trying to fool myself.

Our bedroom looked all hazy, what with the sleep still in my eyes and my glasses on the dresser. The light from the hall cast ugly shadows. It was so hot and stuffy that I thought somebody had put a plastic tent over my bed. My mind didn't want to sleep any more and my body didn't want to wake up. I didn't move for a long while.

When I got to the bathroom mirror to look at myself, I decided I was definitely getting older. I had to. With everybody else crying or cracking up I just had to toughen up. Like Dad used to say, "When the going gets tough, the tough get going." The Bloop used to say, "Yeah, but where do they go? Probably to as safe a spot as they can find." Sometimes the Bloop is wilted.

I got Jimmy up and shook my mother out of her sleep on the couch. Shelley was walking around upstairs so I figured I could leave for school.

My body felt heavy, as if gravity had gone crazy and the earth was trying to suck me into it. My legs didn't move as fast as they usually did, my arms hung down and felt awkward. I guess I hadn't slept very well. A headache was inching across my forehead. I figured I'd get some aspirin from the nurse when I got to school.

Crazy Charlie was down at the Circle before I got there. I hadn't made up my mind whether I wanted to see him or not when he came toward me.

"G-good morning." Charlie held out his hand for me to shake. I left his hand hanging in the air. Charlie looked cruddy. His coat was spattered with salt from the road and there was some birdshit on one shoulder. His cap sat crooked on his head and made him look like a retard. God knows where he got his gloves.

"H-how are you t-today," he said, continuing the routine.

"Not good, Charlie."

"That's t-too bad. That's too bad."

"Yeah."

"Maybe you need s-some advice. Some ph-philosophy." He wiped his dripping nose with his glove.

"Shit. The one thing I don't need is more of your philosophy. You're crazy, Charlie. You know what I mean, crazy. Up there. I don't need crazy advice. I . . ."

I stopped when his mouth fell open. There was a look in his eyes like a dog you accidentally hit on the nose. I turned and walked away. I should have apologized. I said to myself right then, you should turn around and apologize. But I didn't. The gravity got heavier.

When I got to school I went up the north stairs. Usually I took them two at a time. Usually. Up at the first landing I could see Ron Masten. I thought for a second that I should turn around and go back to the first floor. There were other staircases, and who needed any more problems? Then I thought some more and decided, why not. I was already going up the stairway and it's a free country and I've got to start getting tough sometime. Besides, he might be looking for somebody else.

"Hey, Specs."

"What do you want, Ron?" I felt the muscles in my lower arms tighten.

"A little talk."

"About what?"

"Like I hear you been seeing Samantha."

"So what?"

"So is it true?"

I thought for a second about my answer. I could lie, but I knew that he knew the truth. I could simply say yes, but that would seem wilted. Or I could tell him what I thought and see what happened.

"None of your business, shithead."

"You watch your mouth when I talk to you." His hand reached out to grab my shirt. I knocked it away with my arm and could feel some pain shoot up from my wrist.

"Keep your hands off me," I shouted. I was loud because I was nervous, also because I didn't feel like getting pulverized without witnesses. I was in luck. I could hear somebody move toward the staircase from the second floor. So could Ron.

"Don't get all excited, Specs. I don't want to start my day with dirty hands." Old Mrs. Anderson was looking down at us. "I was just thinking that maybe you're spending too much time with your new friend. If you get my meaning."

"Shit."

I flew up the stairs. Past Mrs. Anderson, who was staring at me and about to say something. Past a couple kids I didn't know who were just staring.

My heart was really beating when I got to my locker. I could feel my wrist ache where I had knocked it against Ron. I was shaking. The first two times I tried my combination I couldn't get the lock to open. I was just starting a third try when Mrs. Edelstein came over.

"Danny, that lock is not an approved lock."

I'm going to tough it out, I said to myself. Just tough it out.

13

The phone rang about four o'clock and Shelley answered. A second later she yelled for me, "It's for you, lover boy."

"What?"

"It's your girl," she said with a smile.

I raced over to the phone, kicking up the edge of the carpet as I went and almost falling into Jimmy's model collection. I tried to answer the phone in the sexiest voice I could.

"Helloo."

"Danny?"

"It's me."

"You sound different over the phone."

"I guess so. Geez, I've had a rotten day. How come you weren't in school today?" I pulled the phone off its little table so it crashed to the floor as I tried to sit down.

"I felt lousy. I managed to convince my mother I was coming down with the flu so she let me stay home. I wasn't really sick, you know, but sort of icky. What happened to you?"

"Everything. My father walked out on us last night."

"Oh, no."

"Yeah. I don't know, maybe it's the best thing." I looked to see if Jimmy was around. "I don't think he's coming back this time."

"That's awful."

"Kind of."

"How do you feel?"

"I don't know. I've been more worried about my mother and Jimmy, I really haven't had time to feel anything. No, that's a lie. To be honest, I've felt sort of guilty."

"Uh-hunh."

"But as soon as I start feeling guilty I say to myself that I'm not being fair to myself. You know, I'm really no worse than most other kids. I know I didn't have as much to do with it as Shelley. But that's not fair to her. What can I say? I'm at war with myself. One part of me feels guilty, the other part says that I'm innocent. I guess I'm just confused."

We kept on talking for a long time. I'm pretty awkward on the telephone so I don't know if I made myself very clear. We talked a lot about my father leaving and why and how everybody was taking it and what we were going to do next. After we talked that out I told her some of the problems I'd had in school: how I blew a history quiz, how Mrs. Edelstein whined about my lock, how Mrs. Downey caught me drawing on a desk with my pen.

I told her about all the small things in school but I left out the one big problem, Ron Masten. I wasn't sure that what I had done would seem heroic to her. It seemed to me, the farther away I got from it, more and more stupid. Besides, I didn't know how she felt about him. The Bloop had said that Sam and Ron had gone out together once. Or at least that Ron said so. I decided not to say anything about him.

"You want to come over to my house after school tomorrow?" Sam offered on her end of the phone.

"Great."

"My mother says she's going to be off at a meeting."

"Even better," I said. "My only good news all day."

"See you."

"See you."

Sam kissed her end of the line. I didn't know quite what to do, but I saw Shelley watching me so I decided that I'd just hang up. A man's got to preserve a little self-respect.

I was nervous in school all the next day. I knew that Ron was watching me to see how I'd take his threat. It's amazing how you can sit in a class and know that somebody's eyes are looking so hard at your back that if they were lasers you'd have two holes between your shoulders.

I was late getting to my locker at the end of the day. It's not that I was really afraid of being seen by Ron, it's just that I wanted to talk for a second to Major Henry. By the time I got to the hall, most of the kids had cleared out and Ron wasn't in sight. Samantha already had her coat on but didn't look like she'd been waiting very long.

When we got to her house, she hung up my coat and said, "I wish you wouldn't be so jumpy."

"Jumpy?"

"Nervous. I know you've got some problems but you're so nervous you're making *me* nervous." She grinned. I bumped into the umbrella stand.

"Yeah. I guess so." We went to the rec room. "There's one thing about yesterday I didn't know if I should tell you. I guess I should. You see, I've got a little problem with Ron. He's a little jealous."

"So what?"

"Well, he's the sort of guy who'd like to sell my body to the A&P for next week's hamburger. Don't laugh. Really."

"He's all talk."

"I hope so. You know, I don't know if I'm supposed to ask you this so if you don't want to answer you don't have to. OK?" She nodded, so I went on, "I hear you went out with him a little while ago."

I looked her in the eyes. I didn't know what I wanted to see or what I wanted to hear. It really shouldn't make a difference. But it did.

"Well, he did ask me out."

"Yeah . . ." my heart was beating faster.

"And I thought about going out with him for a second or two," she said, playing with her finger around my mouth, "so I said . . ."

"What?"

"How come you want to know?"

"Stop teasing me."

She pulled her hand away. "How come?"

" 'Cause."

" 'Cause why?"

"Geez. Because I like you." She looked at me very quietly for what must have been a long time. "A lot."

Sam smiled. Then she pulled me forward to kiss

her. "Well, for your information," she said, "I told him I'd rather go out with Alfred E. Newman than waste an evening with *him*."

I laughed. I laughed for the first time in three days. I laughed not because Sam was being funny but because I suddenly felt better.

"You didn't really say that."

"No, I couldn't. I just said that my mother wouldn't approve of him so we couldn't go out. A pretty lame excuse, but he's so icky."

"Yeah."

"And you're so nice."

"Really?"

"Really."

It's amazing to me how, when two people want to kiss, their bodies somehow go together in a sensible way. I used to worry a lot about what to do with parts of my body: where do you put your hands, how do noses fit together, what if she wears braces? I mean, if you consider all the possibilities, it's amazing that people kiss at all. But when it actually comes down to doing it, when you're with a real girl and not practicing on a pillow, everything seems to fall into place. Everything except glasses.

"Hey, you left a nose print on my glasses." When I'm really close to Sam I can see the smoothness of her cheeks and the little wrinkles around her eyes.

"Maybe we should stop." She grinned at me, teasing.

"Well, I didn't say that. I'm just getting smudged."

"Then take them off, dummy."

I did and we kissed again. I felt her hand touching the hair just above my neck. Our tongues met. I could feel her breath coming quickly against my cheek. I pulled her tighter to me and wrapped my legs into hers so she could feel my excitement.

The fingers of my hand moved up under her shirt and felt the softness of the skin of her back. The fingers traced their way up the ridges of her spine. They played with the smoothness of her back while our mouths played with tongues, lips, and teeth. The fingers started fooling with the strap of her bra.

I call them the fingers, not *my* fingers, because they weren't really under my control. I'm not a rapist or anything and, when it comes down to it, I'm only fourteen. But the fingers started trying to undo the strap. They were twisting the hooks, twisting and turning. I think they worked on the hooks for a good five minutes and all that time I was sure Sam would tell them to stop.

But Sam didn't say anything. Her breath seemed to be coming from deeper down and her own hands kept on playing with my neck and my back. Then the most amazing thing happened.

"Wait a minute," she said, sitting up. She slipped her arms around her back, fiddled for a second, and then settled back into my arms.

When the fingers found their way under her shirt again, the strap was free and they moved wildly up and down her back. I could feel my own breathing come more quickly now. And a funny tightness was starting in my chest.

The fingers started moving again. They followed the ridge where the strap had been, around under the dampness of her arm. Then they hesitated for a second, scared I think, building up courage. They moved on over even softer skin.

Sam's lips separated slowly from mine. She took her hand and pulled mine away. I looked at her with a question in my eyes.

"Not now," she answered.

"Unhhh."

"Not now. It's not right yet." In a second she was up on her feet and straightening herself out. "You wanna watch TV?"

And we did. We saw the second half of an after-school movie. Sam made some popcorn which made our little kisses all buttery. My body gradually returned to normal.

On the way home, I was singing the theme music from the movie and was pretty close to skipping down the street. Magic. I couldn't believe how good I felt, how absolutely fine. Back there, caring for me, is a girl who says "Not now," instead of no.

14

Ups and downs. I can't get over how a person's life can be so boring for months at a time and then go crazy all of a sudden. It was two days before the Christmas break. Good. Ron Masten's dinosaur-sized brain knew that I was still seeing Samantha. Bad. I was still seeing Samantha. Good. She was going to Florida over the vacation. Bad. I was passing everything except geography, which I hate. Pretty good. I was sent to the office twice. Bad. My father hasn't come back. That may be good or bad. Geez.

I came up to the Circle on the way to school and saw Crazy Charlie twirling around, throwing birdseed out for his friends. At first I wanted to avoid him by going around the block, then I thought it might be better to go up and apologize. While I was trying to decide, he stopped twirling and waved to me. That was enough to make up my mind.

"Charlie, I'm sorry about the other day, you know. . . ."

"Think no-nothing of it, my man. It's Chr-Christmas. Sh-should old ac-acquain-acquaintance be for-forgot," he finally got out, extending his hand to me.

Christmas was still a week away, but Charlie's wild smile showed that this was no time for me to correct him. I went back to our usual routine. "And what is your philosophy today, Professor? What is your Christmas philosophy?"

"Well," he said wiping his nose. "You w-want to know about Chr-Christmas. This is what I say. This is what I say: Chr-Christmas is l-love."

I waited to see if Charlie had anything to add, but that was it. I patted him on the back and said, "You're amazing, Professor."

Charlie kept on repeating "amazing" to himself as I waved myself off to school. I needed some time to think because my mind was really confused. I tried to focus on something simple so I could keep my thoughts under control. I decided to worry about Sam's Christmas present. Now that was a reasonable problem. Unlike my other problems, it probably had a reasonable solution. After setting aside a couple bucks for my mother, I had about twelve dollars to spend on Sam. Not much. I could get her a slinky nightgown like the girls wear in ads on television. No, her mother would have a fit. I could try to buy some jewelry, but I'd never seen her wear any. Then I could always get a bottle of perfume.

"Specs!"

I looked up and outside myself. I was in school. The voice was Ron's. He didn't say anything else, just leaned against a locker and stared at me. I think I was supposed to be scared, but I wasn't. I stared back at him, looked at the dull features on his face, and made a decision. He's not important. Whatever he does, it's not important. I shrugged and walked on to my locker.

I saw Sam between lunch periods. Actually, because we didn't eat the same lunch, I decided to be a little late for my sixth-period class.

"What are you doing here?" Sam asked.

"It's OK. I'll just be a little late to my next class. I had to see you."

"How come?"

"What do you want for Christmas?"

"I really don't need anything. You know, you should probably hold on to your money."

"Oh, come on."

"Well, I don't know. You pick something. Whatever it is, I'll love it."

"Can I come over after school?"

"I've got to go to the dentist and I'm nervous already. How about tomorrow? I've got to get my passport downtown, but I'll be home before you get out of school."

"You don't need a passport to go to Florida."

"I know, dummy. I might be going to Europe this summer."

"Oh, great," a darkness settled on me, "just the sort of news I need to cheer me up."

"Well, how about tomorrow?"

"OK. See you then."

"See you." She blew me a kiss. I hurried off to class not sure whether I felt better or worse.

In math I decided I felt worse. We started doing some graphing after Major Henry did a confused in-

troduction at the board. I finished what I had to do
early and started goofing around. I drew a naked girl
on the graph paper and stared at her for a second.
Then I thought about graphing her. If I could set up
the right equations, I'd have a formula for drawing
naked girls on graph paper. I could write a textbook
and make a fortune.

I had just started figuring her equations when an
eraser hit me in the back of the head.

"Shit."

My swearing filled the quiet classroom like an explosion. Everybody started laughing. I turned around
and saw Ron Masten laughing harder than all the rest
and knew who had sent the eraser.

When I turned back to my desk, Major Henry was
beside me. Who would ever think that an old man
could move so fast? He was staring down at my graph
paper.

"Danny," was all he said at first.

I started turning red. I knew I was turning red and
tried to fight it, which made it worse. If Major Henry
held the paper up, like Mrs. Sporbeck had done to
Gerald Rosen one day, I might as well curl up and
die.

"Danny, would you see me after class please?"

I nodded and pushed the graph papers together so
that my assignment was on top. He smiled a bit and
went back to his desk. I heard somebody laughing at
the back of the room.

After class was also after school since math was the
last period. I just stayed in my desk while everybody
else was leaving and pretended that sitting there was
the most natural thing in the world. The sky outside

the windows had heavy, dark clouds but the falling snow made the trees and roofs look pretty.

"Danny." Major Henry came over to me after everybody had gone out.

"I'm sorry I swore," I jumped in. "I know you're mad. But somebody hit me in the head with an eraser and it just slipped out. You know? And I was really working on my math. Sort of. I know what you think but it wasn't like that. You see, I was thinking that if I could get the right equations to do her, uh, parts, then I could set up some formulas so that you could, you know, graph a girl. So you see . . ."

"Danny, relax. I'm not that concerned about your language or about the girl on the graph paper."

"You're not?"

"No. I'm concerned about you more generally." He stared out the window at the snow. "I saw in the office that you'd been sent down twice. That isn't like you. Mrs. Edelstein says you've been acting peculiarly lately. Even I've noticed it, Danny, and everybody knows that I'm senile."

"Oh, no, sir."

"Come on. What's the problem?"

"Well, it's at home, mostly."

"Your parents have a fight?"

"Worse. My dad's walked out. They didn't even argue much. He just packed up his stuff and left. We haven't seen him since."

"Have you told anybody?"

"Just the Bl-Myron Rabinowitz and Samantha."

"Oh. How long have you been going with her?"

"How did you know?"

He just grinned and turned his face toward the window. All the lines in his face were exaggerated by the light. He stared at something out in the roofs and trees that I couldn't see. "You know, Danny, you're going through a difficult period right now and what I'm going to tell you isn't going to make any difference. But I'm going to tell you anyhow.

"Right now your life's going up and down like crazy. Things are rough. Things are great. One minute it's suicide. The next it's magic. Often your life seems so difficult and unpleasant that you say to yourself, 'My God, when will this be over?' And it will be over, soon enough. Too soon. Your life will go back to the dull plod, you'll walk nice and steady, everybody will say what a sensible person you are. But you'll be bored. You'll desperately want to be in love again, or in sorrow, or in trouble. Because that's what gives living its *frisson*."

I shook my head.

"Its excitement, its texture. Ultimately, you have to learn to accept the various textures of life. You're learning that now and that's good. When your life's done you can look back on moments with texture and the moments that had none and say to yourself, 'Those moments were beautiful, those had value.' Do you understand?"

I nodded.

"Good night. Merry Christmas."

I left the room with Major Henry still sitting on the desk top looking out at the snow.

15

I made myself a peanut butter and jelly sandwich for lunch at school and started looking for the waxed paper. I found twenty pots and pans, five cans of beans, two cans of cream of asparagus soup which everybody hates, and an empty Nestle Quik can, but no waxed paper. It's a sign that your house is falling apart when nobody remembers to buy any waxed paper. I ended up wrapping my sandwich in newspaper. By lunch time I'd have "Peace Talks Bogged Down" printed on the bread.

I put my sandwich in a brown bag and went up to my room. In the desk, under a Captain Marvel comic, I had hidden Sam's perfume. Actually it was cologne. Looking at perfumes, I found that twelve dollars would only buy something like Essence of Urinal so I settled for a cologne and got her White Shoulders. My wrapping job, I noticed, wasn't the best. It looked like the Hulk had tried to do the job while racing between the swamp and the teleporter. Too late to do it again. I packed the gift in with my lunch.

When I walked past Shelley's room, I wondered if I should tell her about the waxed paper. She hadn't gotten up yet so I guessed that she wasn't going to school. She still hadn't gotten used to my father's leaving and seemed to blame herself a lot. She even broke off with Mangy Bob after a long, angry phone call. If anybody had problems worse than mine, Shelley did. I decided to let her sleep.

The morning at school was dull, "lackluster," to borrow a word from Mrs. Sporbeck's weekly vocabulary list. It was one of those days when a haze seems to have settled down over everyone and everything.

In biology, the Bloop and I started to work dissecting a frog. The assignment in the lab book seemed pretty easy. You slit the thing down the middle and cut out these squiggly things inside to make up a display. The teacher passed out our dead frogs from a huge jar and the whole room stunk of formaldehyde. I wondered if you had to put up with a stink like that at the morgue.

I pinned the frog down as carefully as I could with the Bloop whispering terrible religious jokes to me. Whenever the Bloop and I team up, he gives the orders and makes the jokes while I do the work. It doesn't seem fair.

"Here, you pin this leg down. Why should I be the only one to stink of formaldehyde?"

"Because I am an intellectual, Danny, and you are lumpen proletariat."

"Oh yeah? I'll give you a lumpen."

He just laughed and I pinned the last leg down. Bloop kept on looking at these magnificent transparencies in the book as I did the cutting. Each transparent sheet showed a different layer of stuff we were supposed to find as we cut. All the parts in the book were nicely colored, neatly laid out, and carefully labeled.

When I cut open the real frog the thing was a mess. Everything was swimming in goo. The little parts and squiggles which looked so clear in the book were all jumbled together in the green-brown slime.

"Yecch," said the Bloop, looking over.

"It looks like my dinner last night."

"We must have a defective frog."

"How can you tell?" I asked him. I stared at the frog, looking for where nature had made an error. I figured that since Bloop's father was a doctor he had to know about these things.

" 'Cause the parts don't have their names printed on like in the book."

I didn't even snort at his feeble joke. The frog really was defective. Its parts were all in the wrong layers and either a lot bigger or smaller than in the drawing. It took me a half hour to get most of the little squishy things cut out and placed on the identification sheet. Bloop kept on looking at the transparencies in the book.

"That's what I don't like about books," he said.

"What?"

"They always make life simpler than it really is. I bet there never was a frog in all history that looked like this." He pointed to the perfect drawing in the book. "Someday I want to see a book where the parts are all mixed up and confused and ugly just like real life."

I didn't have time to agree. Ron Masten came stroll-

ing up from the back of the room. When he came up
to our desk, he knocked the identification sheet to the
floor with a quick turn of his hips. The little squishy
parts went flying.

"Oh, I'm so sorry," he said, with obvious exaggera-
tion.

For a second I was stunned. I stared at Ron. I
stared at the mess on the floor. I stared back at the
smirk on Ron's face. My hand closed around a dissecting tool and the muscles in my arm tightened. My
mind was trying to decide what to do, whether or not
this was important, but my hand had made a decision
much faster.

"Easy, Danny," Bloop said reaching over and taking
hold of my wrist. I dropped the tool as the teacher
came up. Bloop did the talking.

Ron maintained his innocence, Bloop talked about
student responsibility. The teacher cut it all off by
giving us an A on what he had seen and lecturing Ron
on being more careful. I still wasn't happy.

"Stop frowning, you're making the frog wilt."

"That shithead."

"You're right, but it doesn't matter. We got a better
mark with the dissection on the floor than we would
have if we handed it in. What's the big deal? When
life hands you a lemon—"

"Make lemonade," I finished as the bell sounded. I
tried hard to be philosophical but it wasn't working so
well. The hand that had grabbed the dissecting tool
was part of me too.

I ate lunch alone. My hands still smelled of formaldehyde after two washings. I didn't even notice
whether the newspaper ink had come off on the
bread. I was looking around at my so-called fellow

students and I felt sick. Under the food-stained ceiling
they all seemed gross: biting a hamburger so the ketch-
up squished out, chewing with their mouths open,
swigging pop so it dribbled out the sides of their
mouths. The cafeteria monitors walked back and forth
probably wondering what fate had brought them to
patrolling a high-school cafeteria for the minimum
wage. The vice-principal, Mr. Guest, sat over by the
food lines with his eyes on another world. In the cafeteria, at least, he did not use his eyes to see. Maybe
when I get older I'll learn how to be as blind as most
adults.

In the corner of my eye I could see Bloop running
over from the stairway. It took a few seconds to realize that he was in the wrong lunch period. By that
time he was next to me.

"Major Henry's had a heart attack right in his
room!"

There wasn't time to say anything. We raced out the
door and down the steps two at a time. I grabbed the
handrail and spun around the stairway corners onto
the landings. From the noise behind us, everybody
else in the cafeteria was just finding out about it. Mr.
Guest was yelling something over the roar as we raced
down the hall.

There were about twenty kids in front of the doorway to Major Henry's room. Bloop stayed at the back
of the crowd because he could see over their heads. I
had to muscle my way to the front. Maybe I shouldn't
have.

Major Henry was lying flat on the floor. His mouth
was open but not moving. His eyes were wide open. I
saw all this with a glance. But it was his skin that
really told me. It was an awful gray-white, powdery

and lifeless. Mrs. Edelstein was kneeling down by him. She kept on arranging and rearranging a blanket which covered his legs.

I turned away because I started feeling dizzy and sick. My head was warm and my brain was starting to play tricks on me. The first trick it played was hope. I said to myself, old people get heart attacks all the time, they're not usually fatal. I said, they'll revive him as soon as the ambulance gets here, just like on TV. I said, he'll probably be teaching again in no time.

The second trick my brain played was making it hard for me to stand up. I let my body lean into the crowd and they seemed to hold it up. I couldn't do it myself.

Other teachers finally came in, followed by the ambulance attendants. I thought it took them forever to come, though Bloop said later that the ambulance was there within five minutes of the call.

We were forced out into the hall. I couldn't see what was going on inside but other people say it was all useless from the start. I remember Major Henry's body coming out on a stretcher all wrapped up in white. I remember that the white sheets came up over his face. On TV, I said to myself, that means death, but only on TV.

I remember somebody pushing me to my next class. I don't know what went on there because my attention was all inside. I knew that he was dead and I couldn't figure out why it was making me all numb. People die on TV all the time. People die, period, It's not a big deal, I said to myself. I knew I was lying.

The PA announcement closing the school came over near the end of the period. They said that Major

Henry had died before he reached the hospital. They said a few simple things about his work as a teacher and how young people liked him. I can't remember that stuff very clearly now.

I remember that when everybody else went to their lockers I went to the bathroom. I locked myself into a stall and sat down. I started crying. I covered my face with my hands and could smell the stink of formaldehyde.

16

The halls were quiet when I came out. Echoes of my steps bounced off the walls. I clanked open the door to my locker and got out the lunch bag with Sam's perfume. I didn't know what I wanted to do.

I felt like going home and doing nothing. My body was so numb that it seemed useless to go over to Samantha's house. But there was no reason to go home, and I had told Sam that I would see her after school. I tried to sort out what was important. I decided that Sam's waiting for me meant more than my mood or my body's lack of feeling. I checked the wrapping on the perfume and put it in the pocket of my parka.

The snow and wind were blowing in through the battered doors downstairs. I saw the great black gray clouds moving across the sky and felt the cold whipping across my face as I went out. There were only three or four kids left outside. They were moving quickly away from the school like the clouds.

I was near the edge of the parking lot when I got

hit. A snowball landed right in the back of my head. I skidded around on the ice.

It was Ron Masten.

I felt the heat in my body building up against the prickling snow on my neck. I knew that my hands were twitching, too. I was fighting to get control back.

"Hey, Specs."

I stared at him for a second. Then I turned my back and started walking on. My body was getting ready for a fight and wanted to get on with it. But my mind was still in control and knew that it had problems enough. I started thinking to myself to stay cool. If I had learned anything in the last couple of weeks, it was that little-kid solutions to problems wouldn't work. The Hulk was powerless against the intergalactic transporter because he was still a little kid. Ron Masten was acting like a little kid, trying to punch out my relationship with Sam. It wouldn't work. In a funny way, I was more powerful than either Ron or the Hulk because I knew that a fight wouldn't make any difference. It just wasn't important.

"I'm talking to you, Specs."

"Buzz off."

"I said I'm talking to you. I thought I told you to stop seeing Sam. Right? But you don't pay attention. You must be pretty dumb." He grabbed my shoulder.

"Let go."

"I'm talking to you, Specs, and you're gonna listen. Now listen. I don't give a shit about Sam anymore. I couldn't care less about the little bitch. . . ."

"Shut up." I could feel my voice trembling. It was like my whole body, shaking and only half under control. I waited.

"What's the matter? Am I starting to get to you?"

I was burning. The fear and anger in me kept fighting against each other. It wasn't time for a fight. I was breathing funny. I turned sideways.

"Oh, don't get emotional on me. You're all sad that your buddy-boy teacher kicked off. The old fag. Now don't start crying."

I wasn't crying. I wasn't doing anything or even moving. My muscles were so tense I didn't even know if I could move.

"I heard you used to be a tough kid. I don't see it now. How come? Maybe everybody's lying about you. I heard your father walked out on you. Geez, I don't blame him. . . ."

That was enough. I swung at him without looking. My fist landed in his jacket. The padding was so thick I knew it didn't hurt him much. Ron smashed me in the chest and I felt it more than I thought I would. I grabbed hold of him. Somebody yelled "Hit him in the face," and I tried. He grabbed me around the neck and then we were both in the snow.

I lifted both hands up and smashed them into Ron's face. From the grunt I knew I had hurt him. I tried to get up but he caught my leg and I was down again. In a second he was on top of me. I brought my hands up to protect my face and started rocking my body to get him off me. Nothing worked. He kept on pounding me. I was losing.

Somehow I managed to twist and throw him off. We both rolled up against the fence and then he was on me again. I felt his fist hit my face. The pain spread out from where he hit me. My nose and lip felt wet. I tried to cover myself again.

I turned my face over and saw a piece of muffler pipe on the ground about two feet away. I stared at it for a second while Ron's knees pressed into my ribs. He bounced down on me and knocked the air out of me.

That's when I lost control. My mind could take losing the fight and it could take the pain. But my body wouldn't. My hand reached over and grabbed the pipe. Ron smashed into my jaw while I reached out but couldn't stop me. I swung the pipe into the small of his back.

I felt the pipe shake and I could see the pain in Ron's face. I wanted to stop. But I wasn't really in control. My body twisted and Ron fell off on the snow. He seemed stunned. My legs climbed up and pinned his arms. My hands took the pipe and started pressing it into his throat. I kept on telling them to stop but my arms wanted another death. They kept on pressing.

That's when I heard "Stop it!" and then I was lying in the snow. When I looked up I saw Bloop. My arm went loose and my hand dropped the pipe. I felt cold.

❋❋

17

A minute later we were a block from the school, out of breath from running. I grabbed hold of a tree trunk for support. Bloop leaned against a fence and stared at me.

"Geez. You could have killed him."

"Yeah."

He stared at me a little longer as if there were another question he wanted to ask.

"Is he OK, you think?"

"Probably. I saw him get to his feet when we took off."

"Got a handkerchief?"

"Yeah, here."

I tried to clean myself up. My whole body ached and was still shaking from the cold and the fight. I put the handkerchief up to my nose and rubbed at the dried blood. My lower lip felt like it was three times larger than normal. There was blood on it, too.

Bloop started laughing. I gave him a look to see if

his mental marbles were spilling all over, but he
didn't stop. He was bent over double with laughter
and trying to say something at the same time.

"Y-you stink," he finally got out.

"What do you expect?"

"No, that's not what I mean. You smell like perfume," Bloop said, waving his hands. "You get in a
fight with the biggest wilt in school and you come out
smelling like some kind of French perfume. I don't believe it."

It took me a minute to figure out what he was talking about. I lifted my parka up and sniffed at the fab-
ric. At first, all I could smell was the sickly stink of
dirt and blood, then I caught just a trace of something
sweeter. Unmistakable: the White Shoulders I had
bought for Sam.

I looked over at Bloop and saw a huge grin spread
across his face. It made me laugh. My laugh grew bigger and bigger, even though it hurt my nose and made
pain shoot out from my jaw.

Bloop leaned back against a lamppost and smiled at
me while my laughing died into giggles and then into
pain. My nose started bleeding again and drops of
blood fell on the snow. I put the handkerchief up to
my nose and tilted my head back.

"Don't you notice that you're missing something?"
Bloop asked.

I thought for a second that this was just the setup
line for some joke, so I refused to say "No, what?"

"I mean you haven't got your glasses."

"Geez," I felt at my face, "they must be back there
on the ground someplace."

"We better go back."

Bloop and I walked back to the edge of the parking

lot. There was no one around. The wind was blowing across the open lot, patches of sunlight mixed with the dark shadows of clouds on the snow.

Bloop bent over and searched the ground in case the glasses were buried in the snow. I backed away and tried to see the whole area at once. I couldn't see very well close up anyhow.

"I got 'em," Bloop yelled.

My glasses were in the snow maybe ten feet from where I stood. When Bloop went out to pick them up, I thought for sure they'd be smashed. I was wrong. Bloop handed them to me and I saw that the frames weren't even bent. I wiped the snow off with my glove and put the glasses back on.

The ground popped into focus. I saw the snow, packed and dirty, under my feet. The rusty muffler pipe was lying a few feet away. There were small drops of blood all over the snow and some broken glass pushed flat in the white surface. I looked up and saw Bloop watching me as if I were one of his father's patients.

"Hey, I'm OK," I said.

"You look sort of funny to me, still. Suppose I walk you home just in case you pass out on the way," he offered.

"I'm not going home. I told Sam I'd come by her house after school and bring her Christmas present. She's probably wondering where I am."

"Look, your Christmas present is busted all over you, and your coat, and the ground. Your face looks like you got the Hulk to do plastic surgery. Are you sure you still want to go see Sam?" He gave me the sort of look he usually saved for Crazy Charlie, half-mocking and half-serious. I didn't like that expression and just stared at him until he looked away from me and dropped the smile from his face.

"I'm going to Sam's," I said quietly.

Bloop shrugged his shoulders and waited for me to start walking out of the parking lot. The wind had died down and so had our talk. It must have started snowing again during the fight. Fresh snow was shining on top of the sooty leftovers from the last storm. It made a kind of white dust around our boots as we walked.

At Samantha's house I rang the doorbell while Bloop stood back by the gate. Sam opened the door and stood perfectly still when she saw me. We all seemed frozen for a second while she read the story of the afternoon in my face.

"Danny."

She reached out and took hold of me.

18

Sam took me down to the rec room after waving
Bloop off and drawing me into the house. She made
me lie down on the couch and then started buzzing
around, looking for things in the medicine chest.

She came back beside the couch with enough medi-
cal stuff to stock the average drugstore. I watched her
dump the stuff beside the couch and then lean forward over me.

"This'll hurt," she said.

It did. She put Mercurochrome on a cut under my
nose and on another at the corner of my mouth. I
creased my forehead from the sting of the medicine
and then relaxed back into the couch pillow.

"Now drink this."

I took a sip from the small glass she held forward to
me and felt heat rush to my throat. I started coughing
and wondered what kind of poison she had in the
glass.

"It's whiskey," Sam said. "That's what they always drink on TV after they've been in a fight."

"Yeah, and just before they amputate. What are you going to chop off?"

"Just your head. The rest of your body still looks pretty good," she smiled.

Sam took a warm cloth and rubbed at the dirt and bits of dried blood on my face. When she was finished, she looked me over as if I were a frying pan she'd been cleaning with a Brillo pad. I must have passed inspection because she started picking up the stuff she'd brought from the medicine chest.

"What's your mother going to think of all this?"

"She's off touring some old houses with a busload of other snobs," Sam said. "But don't start getting any ideas. You've got to take it easy."

I laid back on the couch and tried to take it easy but knew that I couldn't. My mind was racing out of control, back to the fight, to Major Henry lying white and dead on the floor, to my father standing with a suitcase in each hand. I tried to focus and get control back.

I saw Sam's face hovering a few inches from mine. The glow from the fireplace at the far end of the room made Sam's skin a very soft pink. The color seemed to touch her cheeks so effortlessly and then disappear into the shadows around her eyes and mouth. The lights from the Christmas tree gave color to Sam's hair, somehow trapped in the blond strands, getting free in little sparkles of light when she moved.

My mind clicked back to why I was to be here.

"What's the matter?" Sam asked, reading my face again.

"Your present."

"Uh-hunh."

"It got broken in the fight."

"It doesn't matter."

"It matters to me. I got you this nice bottle of White Shoulders and had it wrapped up and everything. But it was in my coat pocket and got smashed during the fight with Ron. Afterwards, the Bloop started laughing at me because I smelled like perfume."

"He's funny. So are you."

"But it was your present and I haven't got anything else to give you."

Sam didn't say anything. She bent over and buried her face in my neck. I felt warmth moving from the base of my spine out into my body. The warmth made my muscles tighten and my breathing go all funny.

"Sorry," Sam said as she sat up again. "I shouldn't do that. You're supposed to relax."

"But I don't want to relax."

"I've still got a couple presents for you," she said, sidestepping what I wanted. "I'll go get them."

A second later she was back with two boxes. One was about three feet long and wrapped in tissue paper, the other was pretty small and covered with gold foil. Sam carried both boxes in and laid them down beside the couch.

"I knew this first present was right for you when I bought it. But this last week I started to change my mind so I got the little one. Never mind why, just open this first," Sam said, holding the big box out for me.

"Do I have to guess what it is?"

"You wouldn't have a chance. Open it."

I tried to take the tissue paper off neatly by pulling the tape at the ends. At our house, we always just ripped at the paper and left the shreds on the floor, but I didn't want to act like a slob in front of Sam. It took forever to get the tissue unwrapped and some of it ripped anyway before I uncovered a large white box. I pulled off the lid. Inside was the Hulk.

"Isn't he great?" Sam laughed, clapping her hands.

I just stared at the doll. It lay scowling in the box, a soft, green figure bursting out of its clothes. I tried to keep a straight face while Sam giggled, but a smile won out over my embarrassment.

"How'd you know about me and the Hulk?"

"I heard you bribe Jimmy that day I was at your house."

I wasn't sure what to say. I always thought that the Hulk routine I had worked up for Jimmy was a little wilted. Looking up at Sam, I still wasn't sure how she felt.

"The Hulk's really great for a little kid like Jimmy," Sam said without my asking. "And I can just see you playing the part, with a deep Hulk-voice and everything."

"Yeah, it's great for a little kid."

"But that's not your real present," Sam said, picking up the small box. "This is."

I pulled off the bow stuck to the gold wrapping and carefully unfolded the paper at one end.

"Nice paper," I said.

"Oh, go ahead and rip it."

"Gotta admire the texture, you know," I said, rubbing my fingers over the paper. "Here it comes." I slipped the box out from its wrapping and held it up: Pierre Cardin cologne.

"Oh, my. Should I put some on?"

"Uh-hunh. I think you'll like the scent better than that old stuff you use. This is . . . uh . . . sexy."

I smiled at Sam and then took the bottle out of its box. Splashing a little cologne on my neck, I lay back on the couch.

"How's that?"

"Irresistible."

I pulled her face down to mine and kissed her gently, the surfaces of our lips just barely touching.

"Wait," she whispered. Sam lifted her head slightly, then slipped my glasses off with one hand and put them on the lamp table.

"Hey, I need those," I said, starting to rise up.

"What for?" Sam smiled at me, holding me down.

"Well, I gotta see things."

"You've seen enough for now," she said, climbing on the couch next to me.

YOUNG LOVE

IS A VERY SPECIAL FEELING